KING OF *Diamonds*

KING OF *Diamonds*

by

C.L. LOWRY

CREEDOM PUBLISHING COMPANY

Published by Creedom Publishing Company

This book is a work of fiction. Names, characters, places, and incidents either are products of the author's imagination or are used fictitiously. Any resemblance to actual persons, living or dead, events, or locales is entirely coincidental.

The Cataloging-in-Publication Data is on file at the Library of Congress.

creedom

ISBN: 978-1-946897-17-6

Printed in the United States of America
10 9 8 7 6 5 4 3 2 1

Dear Reader,

Welcome to the captivating series of The Street Kings, where the boundaries of traditional storytelling are deliberately blurred. I want to guide you through a remarkable literary experience that invites you to explore the narrative in an unconventional way.

Within the world of the Street Kings, I have intentionally crafted a novella series of interconnected stories that defy the conventional norms of sequential reading. Each book in the novella series is an independent tale, a self-contained universe brimming with its own characters, mysteries, and adventures. These books are designed to be enjoyed as individual gems, offering a unique and satisfying journey with every read.

Embrace the freedom to dive into the world of the Street Kings at your own pace, without the constraints of a traditional fixed reading order. Feel free to follow your instincts and choose the book that calls out to you. Whether you begin with the Queen of Hearts or venture into the depths of the King of Diamonds first, each entry in the novella series promises a complete and fulfilling narrative experience.

I intend to empower you, the reader, to curate your own path through this literary tapestry. As you navigate through the tales within this series, you will uncover threads that connect the stories in unexpected ways. The choice of the sequence is yours, and I hope you will relish the excitement of piecing together the larger picture as you embark on your journey and prepare for *King of the Streets 2*.

So, heed this disclaimer as an invitation rather than a caution. Embrace the freedom to explore, wander, and be pleasantly surprised by the intricate web of storytelling in each book. With each story, you are embarking on a fresh adventure, a new perspective, and an opportunity to savor the series in a way that resonates uniquely with you.

Thank you for choosing to experience this series in all its unconventionality. Prepare to be immersed in a world where order is not essential, discovery knows no bounds, and the joy of reading comes alive in extraordinary ways.

-

Prologue

PREVIOUSLY IN *KING OF THE STREETS*...

The door to the large storage locker was pulled up, and a dim light was on in the corner. Nicolás Muñoz entered the locker and closed the door behind him. He was dressed in a tan Kiton suit, white dress shirt, and Mezlan crocodile shoes. The odor of bloody flesh filled the small area. Nicolás removed his suit jacket and draped it over a chair that in the corner of the room. The odor bounced around Nicolás' nostrils. The scent was intoxicating to him. Nicolás loosened his tie and rolled up the sleeves of his dress shirt. He walked toward the center of the storage locker, toward a naked man that was curled up in the fetal position on the ground. The man was lying in a pool of his blood. Deep lacerations covered his face and body. Four men stood in each corner of the storage locker, each of them in possession of machetes.

"El hijo de puta," Nicolás muttered before spitting on the man. He hovered around, circling the man like a vulture in the sky. "Esto es lo que hacemos a las serpientes," he announced proudly.

Although the sight before him pleased his dark soul, he wasn't happy about the reason behind the man's unforeseen fate. Treachery had reared its ugly head.

Nicolás grabbed a crate from the corner of the storage locker and placed it just above the male's head, before sitting on it. His heartbeat was steady, his palms were dry, and there was no expression on his face. He felt betrayed but didn't show it. The man that he rested his eyes on was once considered an ally, and now it was time to cut all ties with the traitor.

"I guess you didn't think we were going to find out," Nicolás whispered into one of the bloody ears before pulling out a stack of papers that he had rolled up in his back pocket. He threw the papers down at his feet, just in the line of sight of the man's swollen eyes.

"You know what this is? These are the cell phone records from my sons, from the week they went missing. Guess who was the last person they contacted?" There was no response except groans as the pain from the man's wounds began to worsen. "You were texting and calling Alejandro on the same night that I last heard from him. Did you kill my sons, la perra?"

"I di—didn't do this."

SMACK!

"Cállate," Nicolás growled after backhanding the man in the face. "Don't you fuckin' lie to me!" Nicolás closed his eyes for a brief moment. He couldn't help but think about his boys. "Do you know how hard I tried to keep my boys away from this lifestyle? I also tried to keep my daughter away, but they all want to be a part of all of this craziness. My boys didn't find out what I did for a living until they were teenagers. As soon as they found out what I was involved in, they immediately wanted to sell drugs. Do you believe that? They were rich and they aspired to be corner boys. My biggest mistake was raising them in America and not Colombia. They were fascinated with all this Hollywood bullshit. They wanted fame over money, and that is dangerous. They wanted to be known. It is better to move in silence because the more noise you make, the more trouble you invite into your world; trouble like you. I allowed them to be distributors so they would be safe. I thought I could keep them safe. Tell me what you did with my sons."

"I didn't —"

SMACK!

Nicolás backhanded Ramir in the face a second time. The lion's head ring he was wearing left a bloody imprint on Ramir's cheek.

Nicolás reached into his pocket and pulled out a tool. He grabbed Ramir's left hand and positioned his pinky finger between the blades of the pruning shears. Nicolás expected Ramir to begin begging at this point, but the young street soldier was molded to withstand his current situation. Nicolás slowly squeezed the handle of the shears, watching the blades slice into the finger.

"ARRRRGGGHHH!" Ramir screamed at the top of his lungs as Nicolás began to dismember his hand. One by one, Nicolás took away the fingers off both hands. Ramir's screams sent a chill down Nicolás' neck. The young soldier began to fade in and out. He was losing too much blood.

"Uhhh. Th—they weren't who you think they were." Ramir spit out a large glob of blood.

His body ached, and each laceration burned to his core. A stabbing pain in his torso left him balled up on the ground, as a result of several broken ribs. He was so weak and battered; he could barely lift his head to look at Nicolás. The swelling around his eyes blinded him, and the blood that filled his broken nose made it nearly impossible to breathe. This had been the first time Ramir was ever in this type of position. He had always been a hunter, and now he had become the hunted. Even after covering their tracks by disposing of the bodies, cell phones, and vehicles of the Muñoz brothers after killing them, Ramir made one grave mistake. He called them from a traceable number that came back to him, so once Nicolás pulled the phone records, he was able to put the pieces of the puzzle together.

"Where are my sons? Are they alive?"

Ramir coughed up another glob of blood. "I don't know."

"Stop lying. Did your bosses make you do this? Did Cristóbal give you the orders to kill my sons?"

Ramir gathered the last bit of energy he had left. "Fuck you."

Nicolás thought long and hard about anyone who could have been involved in the disappearance of his sons. The Street Kings were the last crew he expected to betray him, especially because the crew was making so much money off his product. There was so much disbelief. Cash even agreed to assist him in the search for his sons. However, since he felt as though The Street Kings had betrayed him, he was ready to send a message. Nicolás grabbed one of the machetes from his henchmen. "Soy el rey de las calles." With one fell swoop, Ramir's head rolled a foot away from his body.

"I'M THE KING OF THE STREETS"

Chapter 1

The jet landed at Morristown Airport and it was time to get down to business. As everyone exited the jet, Don noticed three luxury SUVs waiting for them a few yards away from their current location. Lorenzo and one of his men escorted Don and Dominic to one of the vehicles, a silver Lincoln Navigator. The other men, the guards and the women filled the other two SUVs. Don was a bit relieved that he was no longer being treated like a prisoner. With a pocket full of diamonds, he was actually excited to get started on this operation. Another motivator was repaying his debt to Big Al. Don couldn't help but think about the warning Federal Agent Miles gave him when he was in prison: "*Once Big Al does you a favor, you'll owe him forever.*"

"Get comfortable, we have about an hour ride from here," Lorenzo informed Don.

"Where are we headed?"

"Hamburg. We have a place over there that's all set up for you."

"A place? Why do I need a whole place for a short visit?"

Lorenzo looked back at Don and laughed. Don didn't know how to interpret the laughter. *Something aint right about this shit. I can stay in a hotel and get the job done. Why would they buy a place for me?* He made sure he was observant of the street signs and area, just in case he had to navigate on his own at some point. Besides being taken to the Federal Penitentiary, Don had never been to New Jersey. He couldn't help but think about his family and Ayanna. If they don't hear from him, they are going to turn the city upside down to find him. The only problem is they'll be looking in the wrong city. No one in Atlanta knows about the Italians or Don's trip to Jersey.

The driver cut down the time on the ride to about forty-five minutes. As they pulled onto Bracken Hill Road, Don immediately noticed the massive homes that filled the street. Although the homes were large, each home was built on at least an acre of land or more. There was a ton of space between neighbors. Don lived a great luxurious life, but in the past 24 hours, he had been exposed to an entirely different lifestyle. He was more low-key than Cash, who bought six cars and two mansions. Don was happy with his condo and BMW. He wasn't too flashy because he wanted to stand out in a different way. He wanted to be respected when he walked into a room of millionaires, not hunted down by street thugs who were desperate for a come-up.

The driver pulled into the driveway of the large, five-bedroom home. The landscaping was pristine. The bushes were professionally trimmed, along with the lawn. There was a three-car garage and one of the garage doors was open. Each of the men exited the Navigator. Don adjusted his tie, feeling the weight of his past and future hanging around his neck as he eyed the luxurious New Jersey neighborhood. Marco and Vito flanked him, dressed impeccably in tailored Italian suits that matched the car's elegance.

"Dis is it, Don," Marco said, a grin splitting his weathered face. "Big Al's gift for ya."

"Damn," Don muttered, his eyes scanning the opulence before him. He had come a long way from the grimy streets of Atlanta, but the memories still clung to him like the scent of gunpowder after a firefight. "I'm going to take a look around," Don yelled out as he worked his way around the side of the house. He immediately noticed the cameras that were set up on the corners of the home. Even around the side of the home the bushes and trees looked like they belonged in an arboretum. Don was in such disbelief. Once he reached the rear of the home, he was sold. The in-ground pool with the pool bar and slide were definitely a nice touch. *Big Al don't play no games.* Don sat on the porch and just took in the moment. He took a deep breath of the fresh air and enjoyed the view. It was relaxing.

"Beautiful, isn't it?" Lorenzo asked. He emerged from the side of the home, holding a bag.

"Yea. It actually feels a bit unreal."

"How so?"

"It seems like I don't deserve it. After everything that has happened, I'm just grateful to be alive.

"We all are," Lorenzo said. He began rearranging the patio furniture, sliding the small table in front of Don and putting a chair up to the table. He placed the bag on the table and carefully removed the items. Two sets of house keys, a cell phone, an iPad, a laptop, two prepaid debit cards, a stack of cash, and a black handgun. Don looked around to make sure the neighbors weren't watching and then remembered how far of a distance they were in relation to the home. "So, are you going to explain all of this shit?" he asked.

"These are the keys to the house. The silver keys are for the front door and the gold keys are for the back. You must carry the phone with you at all times because that's the one Big Al will be calling you on. My number is already programmed into it. Unfortunately, we can't allow you to call out or text other people. That would jeopardize this operation."

"What are these for?" Don asked, grabbing the two debit cards and reading the information printed on each of them.

"Those are NetSpend prepaid debit cards for you to use, since we took your cards."

"What's the limit on the cards?"

"15,000."

"How much is on each card?"

"They are both at the maximum limit."

"So, what 'bout this?" Don asked holding up the stack of cash. "I'm gon' tell you just like I told Dominic, I don't want Big Al's money. I don't want to be paid for this. I'm helping him out because he helped me out when we were locked up.

"That's just spending money, just in case the cards don't work for some reason?"

"It's like $50,000 here. If this is spending money, how long do yall expect me to be out here?"

"Listen, man, I'm just following orders."

"So, what's up with the iPad and laptop?"

"I didn't know which one you preferred, so I got both. They are brand new, so you can set them up however you want."

"Where is my phone and wallet?"

"I have them and they are going to be put in one of the safes in the house. Once your mission is complete, you will be given the code to the safe. You also have an extra handgun and plenty of ammo inside the gun locker in the basement. Do you have any more questions?

"Just one, who am I staying with?"

Lorenzo laughed. "You're going to be here by yourself. It isn't necessary to babysit you any longer. Oh, and that reminds me," he said while digging into his pockets. "You can contact this guy about a car. We have a connection to his dealership and he will hook you up with a car, tags, and all the documentation to go with it. I can have the driver take you to the dealership in the morning if you want."

"Yea, that'll be cool.

"Perfect. Marco and Vito will be hanging out for a while. There are also two housekeepers, Jessica and Lucia, that will make sure you eat well and that the home is always clean. If you need anything at all, don't hesitate to let them know."

Lorenzo then headed back to the SUV. Marco and Vito led the way to the front door of the home.

"Damn," Don muttered, his eyes scanning the opulence before him.

Vito swung the door open, revealing a spacious living area bathed in warm light. The plush furniture beckoned, inviting the trio into a world of comfort far removed from the chaos of their respective pasts.

"Make yourself at home," Vito said, handing Don a handwritten note. "Big Al wanted you to have this."

Don unfolded the note, Big Al's familiar scrawl bringing forth a rush of gratitude and loyalty. The two of them had been through hell together, locked up in the same cell, fighting for survival. Now, Don was a free man, thanks to Dominic Ricci, the lawyer whose brilliance had shattered the chains on their lives.

"Welcome to your new life, my friend," the note read. "I owe you more than I'll ever be able to repay. Enjoy your stay and remember—you always have a place here with us. - Big Al"

"Thanks, man," Don said, his voice thick with emotion. "Tell Big Al that I appreciate it."

"Of course," Marco replied, giving him a firm pat on the back. "We'll leave you to get settled. Just holla if you need anything."

With that, the two Italians turned on their heels and disappeared down the corridor, leaving Don to explore his new surroundings. The luxurious home felt like an alien world, so far removed from the grit and grime of the streets he had come to know as home. But this was Big Al's gift to him—a chance at a fresh start, a life unburdened by the shadows of his past.

As Don took it all in, he knew that he would never be able to repay Big Al for the trust and faith he had placed in him. But he also knew that with every fiber of his being, he would do everything in his power to prove himself worthy of this opportunity. And maybe, just maybe, they could build something together—a new empire, free from the treachery and betrayal that had plagued their former lives.

Don's eyes scanned the lavish residence, taking in the plush furniture and sleek modern lines. He sighed, realizing he should feel grateful, but something was off. A nagging thought scratched at the back of his mind. It didn't take long for it to surface—his wallet, phone and personal belongings were still confiscated.

"Damn," Don muttered, rubbing the back of his neck. He felt like a fish out of water without his phone connecting him to the world beyond this swanky home. How was he supposed to keep tabs on his crew or check on his real estate ventures? The walls seemed to close in around him, amplifying his anxiety. Pacing back and forth, he found himself staring at the door, half expecting someone to burst in and put a bullet in his head.

"Get a grip, man," he told himself, tryna shake off the paranoia. "Ain't nobody comin' for you here." Still, without his phone, he couldn't help but feel vulnerable. And vulnerability wasn't something Don had allowed himself to feel in a long time.

"Maybe I can ask Jessica or Lucia if they got a spare phone I can borrow," he thought aloud, remembering the two Italian women who would be working at the home. But then again, he didn't want to seem needy or ungrateful. He bit his lip, conflicted.

"Man, this ain't like me," Don mumbled, running a hand across his head. "I ain't been this rattled since...since prison." That dark time in his life had taught him many lessons, including how to adapt and survive. He needed to channel that same resilience now, even if it meant facing his fears head-on.

"Alright," he said, stepping away from the door. "No more wallowin' in self-pity. If I can make it through prison, I can damn sure handle a little disconnection." Determined, Don focused on the luxury surrounding him, trying to appreciate this new life Big Al had granted him. He'd find a way to adapt, to keep pushing forward—that was the only way he knew how to survive. And maybe, just maybe, he'd learn to be comfortable without constantly checking his phone or scrolling through emails.

"Time to level up," Don whispered, clenching his fists. "I ain't lettin' nothin', or nobody, hold me back."

Don's stomach grumbled, reminding him that it had been a hot minute since he'd eaten. He peered out the floor-to-ceiling windows, spotting Jessica and Lucia setting up a breakfast buffet by the poolside. Steam rose from silver trays, and the scent of fresh-baked pastries lingered in the air, making his mouth water.

"Let's go see what's cookin'," he said to himself, heading towards the patio door. Don could feel the tension leaving his shoulders as the warm sun greeted him, and he couldn't help but admire the sparkling pool reflecting the morning light. Big Al knew how to treat his people right, that was for sure.

"Buongiorno, Don!" Jessica called out, wiping her hands on a towel draped over her arm. Her dark curls framed her face, and her eyes sparkled with genuine warmth.

"Good morning," Don replied, flashing her a smile. "This spread looks amazin'."

"Thank you," she beamed, leading him to a table adorned with a crisp white linen cloth. "Please, have a seat."

"Hey there, Don," Lucia chimed in, her own smile just as bright. "We've got quite a variety here—eggs, bacon, fresh fruit, yogurt, you name it. Any dietary restrictions or preferences we should know about?"

"Nah, I'm good with anythin'," Don answered, taking a seat and eyeing the food hungrily. "I appreciate y'all puttin' this together."

"We're happy to do it," Jessica assured him, dishing up a plate of scrambled eggs and crispy bacon. "The boss wants you to feel at home here."

"Cool," Don nodded, taking a bite of his breakfast. The eggs were fluffy and the bacon cooked to perfection—he'd missed simple home-cooked meals like this. "Tell Lorenzo that he has really outdone himself, but I don't want you ladies working too hard."

"Will do," Lucia said, refilling' his coffee cup with a practiced hand. "Enjoy your breakfast."

As he ate, Don couldn't help but reflect on his journey thus far. He'd come a long way from the streets of Atlanta, and now he was chilling poolside in a luxurious home in Jersey, eating' a feast prepared by two lovely Italian ladies. His life had taken some unexpected turns, but this one - this one was something else entirely.

"Time to get to work," he muttered under his breath, bracing himself for the challenges ahead. With Big Al's backing, Don knew he could conquer whatever obstacles came his way. And maybe, just maybe, he'd find a way to reconnect with his old world.

"Damn right," Don whispered, takin' another bite of his breakfast. "I got this."

The sun glinted off the pool's surface, sending shimmering' reflections dancing across Don's face as he leaned back in his chair. He let out a deep breath and tried to relax, but old memories kept creeping up on him like shadows at nightfall.

"Man," he murmured, thinking about his crew from back in Atlanta – Cash, Ace, Ramir, and even Trey. The faces of the people he'd come up with flickered through his mind like snapshots from a life that was already starting to feel like a dream. They'd been through hell together and had each other's backs no matter what.

"Shit," Don sighed, picking idly at his plate. Being in prison had changed everything. It had been a wake-up call, and it seemed like every minute of it was etched into his soul. There were moments of laughter, sure, but also moments of darkness he'd never forget – the clang of metal bars, the cold concrete floor beneath his feet, and the way time seemed to stretch out before him like an endless desert.

"Shit," Don whispered, shaking his head. It was hard not to feel a sense of regret, even as he sat there enjoying the warm sun on his face and the finest breakfast he'd eaten in years. He'd made mistakes and paid the price, but he was free now, and that was something to celebrate.

Just then, the click of heels on concrete caught Don's attention, pulling him from his reverie. Ain't no way he could miss Isabella – she stood out like a diamond in the rough. Her sleek dark hair fell in waves down her back, and her eyes sparkled like precious stones themselves. She walked with purpose, carrying a small black velvet bag in one hand.

"Hey there, Don," she greeted him with a warm smile, her voice as smooth as silk. "I heard you were up and about. I'm Isabella, Big Al's gemologist and personal shopper."

"Nice to meet you, Isabella," Don replied, his eyes drifting from her gorgeous face to the velvet bag. Curiosity gnawed at him like a hungry dog. "What you got in there?"

Isabella smiled, opening the bag just enough to give Don a tantalizing glimpse of what lay within. "A little somethin' special from Big Al, but that's for a little later," she teased, closing the bag again. "For now, enjoy your breakfast and relax. You've earned it. I'll be back in a few to talk business."

Don nodded, his curiosity piqued but his patience intact. He watched as Isabella sashayed away, the sun lighting up her features like an angel in disguise. *Yeah*, he thought, *things had definitely changed*. But maybe, just maybe, they'd changed for the better.

Don finished his breakfast, his mind still churning over the memories of the past, when Isabella approached him again. She had that black velvet bag in her hands, ready to reveal its contents.

"Big Al wanted me to give you this," she said, her eyes sparkling with intrigue. Carefully, she opened the bag and tipped out five exquisite diamonds onto the glass table beside Don's plate. Each diamond shone in the morning sunlight, their colors vibrant and cuts so precise they looked like they'd been sculpted by a god. They were much larger than the ones Lorenzo gave to him on the flight.

"Damn," Don murmured, leaning closer to get a better look at the gems. He reached out tentatively, fingers hovering just above the diamonds. "These real?"

"Of course," Isabella replied, a hint of pride in her voice. "Each one is unique in cut, color, clarity, and carat weight. They're all GIA-certified and ethically sourced."

"Big Al got good taste," Don admitted, finally allowing himself to touch one of the diamonds. It felt cool and smooth under his fingertips, despite the heat of the day. He traced its edges and marveled at how it seemed to capture the sun and hold it within its depths.

"Where these come from?" he asked, his curiosity piqued.

"Several different countries," Isabella explained. "The pink one is from Argyle in Australia, the green from South Africa, the blue from Russia, the yellow from Canada, and the white one, well, that's from right here in the US."

"Damn," Don repeated, his gaze flitting from one diamond to the next. "Why Big Al givin' me somethin' like this? I mean, we're tight, but this is some next-level shit. He already gave me some little stones, so why give me these too?"

"Big Al knows loyalty is hard to come by," Isabella said, her eyes meeting Don's. "He appreciates what you're doing for him, and he wants to thank you for your trust."

"Trust," Don echoed, the word hanging heavy in the air between them. He looked back down at the diamonds, each one a symbol of the bond he shared with Big Al. A reminder that despite all the pain and heartache he'd been through, there were still people who had his back.

"I appreciate this more than yall know," he finally said, his voice thick with emotion. "Ain't nothin' more valuable than loyalty and trust."

Isabella nodded, her expression softening. "I agree." She paused, watching as Don continued to examine the diamonds. "And if you ever need anything, Don, just let me know. That's what I'm here for," she said seductively.

"Thanks, Isabella," he replied, smiling up at her. "I'll definitely keep that in mind."

As she walked away, Don couldn't help but feel grateful – not just for the diamonds or his new life, but for the chance to prove himself. The road ahead was long and filled with uncertainty, but with people like Big Al and Isabella by his side, he knew he could face whatever challenges came his way.

The sun blazed high above the pool, the water shimmering like diamonds. Don could feel his skin heating up, but he didn't mind. Nothing beat the feeling of sunlight after being locked away in that cold, dark cell. He was taking in the view when a familiar figure approached from the patio doors – Dominic Ricci, the lawyer who'd fought tooth and nail to get him out of prison.

"Dom!" Don called out, his face breaking into a wide grin. "Didn't expect to see you here. I thought you left with Lorenzo."

"Hey, Donovan," Dominic replied, extending a hand. "Thought I'd come check on you, and see how you're settling in."

Don clasped his hand, giving it a firm shake. "You know me, Dom – always finding my way."

Dominic nodded, pulling up a chair next to Don. "Looks like you landed on your feet. This place is incredible."

"Big Al's treat," Don said with a chuckle. "Just tryin' to make the most of it."

"Speaking of Big Al," Dominic began, leaning in closer, "he told me about those diamonds. He wants you to know they're just the beginning. There's a lot more where that came from if you keep proving yourself."

"Already workin' on it," Don replied, his eyes narrowing slightly. He didn't need anyone to remind him of what he owed Big Al.

"Good man," Dominic said, patting him on the shoulder. "By the way, how's that real estate market treating you? You still flipping those properties?"

"Slowly but surely," Don admitted, rubbing the back of his neck. "It's a tough business, especially after the Feds seize your assets. They are slowly releasing them, but I'll be back in full effect soon."

"Hey, you're a smart guy, Don. I'm sure you'll figure it out."

"Appreciate that, Dom," Don said, his gaze drifting back to the pool. "And I appreciate what you did for me – gettin' me outta there. You stuck your neck out, and I won't forget it."

Dominic smiled, looking' a little embarrassed. "Just doing my job. Besides, we all knew you didn't belong in there."

"Still," Don insisted, "you went above and beyond. Means a lot to me."

"Anytime, Don. If you ever need anything, you know where to find me."

"Same goes for you," Don replied, pulling out a pen and scribbling down his number and email on a napkin. He handed it to Dominic, who did the same.

"Stay in touch, alright?" Dominic said, pocketing the napkin.

"Definitely," Don agreed. "You take care of yourself, Dominic."

As Dominic walked away, Don couldn't help but feel grateful for the people in his life. They'd been through hell together, and somehow, they'd all come out on the other side. Now it was time for him to step up, to show them he was worth believing in. He'd make the most of this second chance – no matter what it took.

Chapter 2

Don stood in the lavish living room of the luxurious New Jersey home, feeling the weight of the diamond in his hand. The sunlight streaming through the floor-to-ceiling windows reflected off the gem, casting a kaleidoscope of colors onto the dark hardwood floors. He knew that Big Al was counting on him to help legitimize his possession of these diamonds and expand his empire. With Big Al behind bars, Don felt an unwavering sense of loyalty to the man who'd had his back during their time locked up together.

"Wow," Don muttered, squinting at the diamond as he turned it between his fingers. "This rock ain't no joke."

He pulled out the phone he was given and quickly snapped a photo of the diamond resting on a black velvet cloth. Then, he scrolled online trying to find a comparable gem. If he was back in Atlanta, he would be able to make one or two phone calls and get a price for the gems on the spot. Now, had to depend on the Italians being the source of his information. He checked the contacts in the phone and stumbled upon Lorenzo's number.

"How much you think this worth?" Don texted, attaching the photo to his message. He hit 'send' and waited for a response, pacing the room with the diamond still nestled in his palm.

"Big Al ain't playin'," Don thought to himself. "We gonna turn these rocks into some real paper, build a legacy for our families."

As he awaited the reply, Don couldn't help but admire the opulence surrounding him. From the imported marble countertops to the plush leather furniture, every inch of the space screamed wealth and power. It was clear that Big Al had made a name for himself in the criminal underworld, and now he wanted to branch out into legitimate businesses, using the priceless diamonds as collateral.

"Shoulda known Big Al had somethin' like this planned," Don mused, remembering the many conversations they'd shared about business ventures and investment strategies while locked up. "Man's always been on another level."

His phone buzzed, drawing him back to the task at hand. He read the message and felt his chest tighten with anticipation.

"The one in that photo, I'd say it's easily worth two million, maybe more," the response read.

"Two milli?" Don murmured, raising an eyebrow as he looked at the diamond again. This was just one of many that Big Al had stashed away, and now it was up to Don to help turn them into legitimate assets.

"Alright, bet," Don replied, pocketing the gem before exiting the room. He knew he had a long journey ahead of him, but if there was one thing he could count on, it was his intelligence and resourcefulness. With those traits in his arsenal, Don was ready to tackle whatever challenges awaited him in the pursuit of Big Al's ambitious vision.

Don walked past the front door, then paused when he heard the knob turning. His instincts kicked in and he ran to the bedroom and grabbed the gun that Lorenzo gave him. Don dropped the magazine from the weapon, confirming it was loaded, then slammed it back into the gun. He was ready for whatever threat that was about to walk through that door.

Don had barely taken a step out of the bedroom when Isabella appeared, leaning seductively against the doorframe. Her dark curls cascaded over her shoulders, framing her flawless face. The way she bit her lip made Don's heart race.

"Hey there, handsome," she purred, her eyes locked on his. "I thought you might need some company."

Don hesitated, torn between his desire for Isabella and his heart still beating for Ayanna. He knew he should walk away, but he couldn't resist the temptation.

"Isabella, you know I was about to put your ass down, right? I wasn't expecting you to come over here."

"I see that," she replied, stepping closer and running a finger down his chest.

"Listen, I'm just here for business."

"But that doesn't mean we can't have a little fun, does it?"

"Damn," Don muttered, struggling to maintain his composure as he felt himself giving in to her advances. "Nobody needs know about this, alright?"

"The secret's safe with me," Isabella whispered, pressing her body against his.

As they moved through the luxurious home, Isabella guided him to a secluded room, dimly lit by flickering candles. She gently pushed him onto the bed, straddling him as she began massaging his tense muscles. Don could feel the weight of his thoughts lifting as she worked her magic. He didn't even know this room existed and was too relaxed to worry about how Isabella managed to get it set up for him.

"Here, try some of this," Isabella said, placing a piece of ripe fruit to his lips. As he took a bite, the sweetness exploded in his mouth, further heightening his senses.

"Damn, girl," Don murmured, savoring the flavor. "You really know how to treat a man."

"Only the best for you, Don," she replied, continuing to feed him fruit between tender kisses.

Their bodies entwined, their passion growing more intense with each touch. Don couldn't help but lose himself in the moment, despite the nagging thoughts of Ayanna at the back of his mind.

"Isabella," he whispered, his voice heavy with desire. "I... I can't do this. My body is saying yes, but my mind wants me to stop this."

"Focus on me, Don," she urged, her breath hot against his ear. "Just for tonight, let yourself be free."

His will to resist was crumbling, his body on fire with desire. And so he did, allowing himself to succumb to Isabella's seduction as they explored each other's bodies. Don leaned in, passionately kissing Isabella and hoisting her on top of him. He felt a sensual heat stirring between her legs, and it was calling his name. At that moment, all thoughts of Ayanna faded away, replaced by the intoxicating allure of the woman that was straddling him.

His body responded instinctively to her seductive touch; the muscles in his neck and back swelled with power. Isabella, dressed only in red lingerie, slid her thong to the side. Now allowing Don access to her pleasurable abyss, she didn't expect the size that was about to enter her body.

Don slid his stiff shaft inside of Isabella, sending her into a frenzy of passion. They both were in a state of euphoria. His pursuit of her felt like an adventure, with each thrust a new thrill. With Ayanna, Don felt she had control over the pace and intensity, but with Isabella, it was almost as if she was guiding him, showing him pleasures he'd never known before.

He gripped her hips, guiding her slow, circular movements. Her ass cheeks rippled as she rode him, sparking a primal desire in him. He wanted to consume her, to have her body as he entered her. His hands gripped her tightly, digging into her flesh as he pushed her deeper onto his manhood.

Don's hands moved to her breasts; kneading them, squeezing them. He pulled her bra down so that he could get a better view of her breasts; a beautiful sight to behold. Her nipples were hard and stiff, and now that he'd released her breasts, he was ready to indulge in them. Don grasped them in his masculine hands, bringing them close to his mouth to suck on them.

"Oh yes!" Isabella moaned, arching her back. Her hands gripped his shoulders, her nails digging into his skin. She groaned with pleasure and she felt him grow harder inside of her.

"Damn, you right there," Don grunted, their bodies slick with sweat. His breathing was short and ragged, his chest heaving as he continued to thrust. He lifted her up, allowing him to penetrate deeper. Her legs wrapped around his waist and he pulled her closer to his anxious body.

"You like this?" he asked huskily, biting her earlobe. "You like feeling me inside that pussy?"

"Yes, yes, yes!" Isabella moaned, the heat between her legs growing to an unbearable level. Her body was on fire and began stiffening as her orgasm overtook her. She twisted beneath Don, her spine bending in ways she never thought possible. She felt her body tighten around Don's dick, gripping him tight.

"That's right!" Don moaned, pumping harder and harder into her. "I'm about to cum in that pussy, baby. You want that?"

"Yes!" she cried.

"Then your pussy better squeeze me tight."

His dick throbbed inside of her as he erupted, spilling his seed inside of the warm abyss. His body relaxed as he enjoyed the feeling of Isabella's pussy. He knew he was leaving something behind, but at the moment, he didn't care. But deep down, Don knew there would be consequences for these actions – though for now, he chose to ignore them.

Lying tangled in the sheets, sweat glistening on their skin, Don and Isabella shared a moment of silence as they caught their breath. The room still smelled of passion and desire, a testament to the intensity of their encounter.

"Tell me something about yourself," Don said, his voice soft and intimate. "Something nobody else knows."

Isabella looked pensively at the ceiling, her fingers tracing patterns on his chest. "I've always wanted to travel the world," she admitted. "See the sights, experience different cultures... but I got caught up in this life, and now it feels like I'll never get out."

"Don't worry, baby girl," he reassured her. "One day you gon' make it outta here, you'll see."

"Your turn," Isabella prompted, turning to look into his eyes.

Don hesitated before answering. "I had a little sister," Don confessed, his voice full of emotion. "She died when we was kids. Sometimes I wonder what kinda man I'd be if she was still around. If I would even be in this game, if I had her in my life."

Before Isabella could reply, Don pulled her close, their bodies reigniting with desire. Their lips fused together, the taste of each other intoxicating and irresistible. Hands roamed, mouths explored, and they were once again lost in each other's embrace. But just as Don reached for Isabella's hips, the sound of the front doorknob turning grabbed his attention.

Don looked at Isabella, wondering if this was something she had up her sleeves. The look of confusion that covered her face let Don know that she didn't know who was at the door. Don threw on his pants and grabbed his gun, stepping out into the hallway and closing the door behind him.

The front door swung open. "Get dressed!" Lorenzo barked, his Italian accent thick and menacing.

Don shot him a glare, his anger flaring at the interruption. "Ain't you heard of knockin', fool?"

"Time is money, Don," Lorenzo reminded him, impatience etched across his face. "And right now, we're wasting both."

"Well, I gotta wash up and stuff."

Lorenzo looked Don up and down, noticing his sweaty body and nervous mannerisms. "I know Isabella came her. Tell her to get dressed too. We gotta go."

Slowly, the door opened behind Don and Isabella revealed herself. Embarrassment was all over her face but in her eyes, it was all worth the risk. The tension in the room was profound as Don and Isabella hurriedly dressed. With one last lingering look, they followed Lorenzo out of the luxurious home and into a waiting black SUV.

As they drove through the streets of New Jersey towards their destination, Lorenzo laid down the law. "Listen up," he began, his voice cold and unyielding. "Big Al's organization don't mess around when it comes to security. You slip up, you get caught by the cops, and it's over for all of us."

Don could feel the weight of Lorenzo's words settling in his chest, reminding him of the danger that came with this life. "I ain't no rookie, man," he countered, trying to keep his voice steady. "I know the stakes."

"Good," Lorenzo replied, his eyes never leaving the road. "Because if you screw this up, it ain't just your ass on the line. It's all of ours."

In the backseat, Don stared out the window, watching the city pass by in a blur. He couldn't help but think about everything he had to lose – Ayanna, his crew back in Atlanta, and now Isabella. The stakes were higher than ever, and as the car sped towards the secret meeting, he knew there would be no turning back.

The black SUV pulled up to a discreet entrance, the dimly lit sign revealing the name of the restaurant: "La Volpe" – The Fox. Don stepped out of the car, taking in the subtle beauty of the exterior. As they entered, he couldn't help but admire the rich dark wood accents and the warm glow of soft lighting that filled the space.

"Damn, this place is nice," Don said, his eyes scanning the room. "Big Al got some good taste."

Lorenzo smirked. "He doesn't own it. It belongs to a friend of his, but it's been closed to the public since the boss' criminal case started. The owner gave me a key and we keep the lights on for him. Now it's strictly used for family business."

Isabella lingered close to Don, her presence still intoxicating. He tried to shake off the lingering sensations from their earlier encounter as they followed Lorenzo to a private booth near the back. They slid into the plush seats, the leather cushions molding to their forms.

"Discreet. I like it," Don mused, trying to focus on the business at hand.

A stunning Italian waitress approached their table, her long dark hair cascading over her shoulders. She carried a silver tray with an old-school corded phone resting on top. Setting it down before Don, she offered him a knowing smile. "Signore, a call for you."

Don raised an eyebrow, exchanging a glance with Lorenzo before picking up the receiver. This was obviously Big Al's doing, wanting to keep a close eye on the situation. He pressed the cool plastic against his ear, waiting for the gravelly voice to come through.

"Yo, Big Al," Don greeted, keeping his tone casual. "What's good?"

In the background, Big Al could hear Isabella and Lorenzo ordering drinks in hushed tones. He knew their conversation could possibly be interrupted by other inmates, so he had to choose his words carefully. The last thing he needed was for someone to know his hand before he played it.

"Hey, Don," Big Al's low, gravelly voice rumbled through the phone. "I ain't gonna beat around the bush. I need your skills and connections, man. You got this gift for making things happen, and I want you on board."

"Appreciate the love, Big Al," Don replied, his eyes scanning the dimly lit restaurant as he formulated a plan in his mind. He could practically feel Big Al's intense gaze on him through the phone. "What exactly you got in mind?"

"Listen," Big Al began, lowering his voice even further. "I got these diamonds, top quality stuff. I need to legitimize them and flip them into physical jewelry stores. Keep it clean and legal, ya know?"

Don's mind raced with possibilities. A jewelry empire would be a game-changer for both of them, but there were other opportunities they could capitalize on as well. "Jewelry stores, huh? That's smart. We could open multiple locations, and generate some serious cash flow."

"Exactly," Big Al agreed. "But I don't want to stop there. I want to diversify my income and bring in more types of businesses. That's where you come in."

"I got you," Don said, catching onto Big Al's vision. His resourcefulness kicked into high gear. "We can also invest in tech, man. There's money to be made in start-ups, apps, all that. It's the future, and we gotta get ahead of it. I knew we rapped about that cryptocurrency shit a while back, but it seems like that's not gonna last long. We need to make investments that have guarantees on the return."

"Damn right," Big Al responded enthusiastically. "That's why I need you, Don. Your knowledge, your connections – we're gonna build an unshakable realm of wealth. But, I need it to be done right. It can't be associated with me in any way on paper. The Feds will be all over it if any of our names are on any paperwork. I need you to find a way to keep it clean and untouchable by the government. We can't use any of my people for this."

The gravity of the situation weighed heavily on Don's chest, yet excitement coursed through his veins. This was the kind of power move that could change his life forever. But at what cost?

"Consider me in," Don said after a moment's hesitation. "Let's get this money."

"Good," Big Al replied, his voice dripping with satisfaction. "I knew I could count on you. Just remember – loyalty is everything."

With that, Big Al remained silent, leaving Don to mull over the implications of his decision. His heart raced as he contemplated the challenges ahead. There was no turning back now.

Don leaned back in his chair; the dim light of the restaurant casting shadows across his face. His mind raced, trying to calculate the risks and rewards of partnering with Big Al. He knew this was an opportunity to make some serious money, but he had his own business to run back in Atlanta.

"Look, Big Al," Don started, his deep voice carrying a hint of hesitation. "I'm down for this plan, but I gotta handle it from back home in Atlanta. I got my own organization to look after."

"Is that right?" Big Al's gravelly voice responded, a tinge of annoyance seeping through. "And what makes you think you can manage my empire from all the way down there?"

Don thought carefully before responding, knowing that one wrong word could end this partnership before it even began. "It's simple, man. I got connections, resources, and most importantly, I know how things work down there. Atlanta's the perfect place to expand your operation."

There was a pause on the other end of the line as Big Al considered Don's words. Finally, he spoke, the tone of his voice leaving no room for negotiation. "Alright, Don. But let's get one thing straight – you either commit to this fully or walk away now. If you're in, you're in for the long haul. There ain't no half-stepping in this game. You give me six months here to get things up and running and you can finish it back home."

Don felt the weight of Big Al's ultimatum bearing down on him, the gravity of the decision pulling him under like quicksand. He took a deep breath, his eyes scanning the luxurious restaurant, searching for answers in the darkness that surrounded him.

"Big Al, I respect your position," Don said, his voice firm despite the turmoil raging inside him. "But I need you to understand that my loyalty to my people in Atlanta is just as strong as my loyalty to you. I can make this work, but I need to do it my way. Six months is a very long time to be away from my folks."

"Fine," Big Al conceded, his voice laced with a warning. "I'll make it a month. But remember this, Don – your loyalty better not waver. If you cross me, there won't be anywhere you can hide."

"Understood," Don replied, knowing full well the consequences of betraying a man like Big Al.

"Good," Big Al grunted before hanging up, leaving Don with nothing but the sound of his own thoughts in the silence that followed.

As Don sat there, the dull hum of the restaurant's air conditioning filling the void left by Big Al's ultimatum, he couldn't help but feel torn. He was a man of fierce loyalty and ambition, caught between two worlds that threatened to tear him apart. But no matter what, he'd find a way to make it work – for himself, for the Street Kings, and for the financial kingdom he was about to help build.

Don sunk deeper into his seat, the plush booth cradling him like a lover's embrace. He stared at the array of expensive dishes on the table, an extravagant symphony of flavors and colors that he'd barely touched. The flickering candlelight cast dancing shadows across the polished marble floor and the faint strains of jazz from hidden speakers provided the perfect backdrop for a night of indulgence.

"Everything good?" Lorenzo asked, his voice a low rumble as he picked at the gold chain around his neck.

Don nodded absently, lost in thought. "Yeah, it's just... this whole situation with Big Al, man. It's got me twisted up."

"Look," Lorenzo said, leaning in closer, his dark eyes serious. "You know as well as anyone else how dangerous Big Al can be. If you don't play your cards right, you could end up six feet under. But I also know you aren't a fool. You've got a plan, right?"

"Always," Don replied, forcing a smile that didn't quite reach his eyes. "I'm just trying to balance my loyalties – to my people and to Big Al. I wanna make sure everyone gets their due without causing any unnecessary bloodshed."

"Bloodshed? Man, you're talking like we are in a war or something," Lorenzo chuckled, but the laughter soon faded when he saw the seriousness in Don's eyes.

"Maybe we would be," Don said quietly, his gaze fixed on the flickering candle flame. "I been in this game long enough to know that every move we make, every decision we take, sends ripples through the streets. And sometimes those ripples turn into waves that can swallow us whole if we ain't careful."

He paused, taking a slow sip of wine, feeling the velvety liquid warm his throat. "Your boss wants to pursue legitimate business opportunities, Lorenzo. Yall can't live this mob life forever. But I also know that I have a responsibility to my people back home, who want the same thing. They deserve to have my time and energy establishing their futures as well."

"Then do what you have to do, man," Lorenzo said, his voice filled with conviction. "I heard you've always been the type to find a way to work out any situation. I trust you'll figure this one out too."

Don nodded, appreciating the support. But as he took another sip of wine and stared out at the city skyline through the restaurant's windows, the question still lingered in the depths of his mind: what would he sacrifice in pursuit of his ambitions?

"Thanks, Lorenzo," he said finally, his voice filled with determination. "I'm gonna make sure it all works out. For everyone."

"Damn right you will," Lorenzo replied, clapping him on the back.

"Let's go," Don said, standing up and leaving the untouched dishes behind, knowing that there was no time to waste. The streets were calling, and he had decisions to make that could change everything – for better or worse.

Chapter 3

Francesco's hands rummaged through Don's personal belongings with a sneer on his face. Francesco is highly ranked in Big Al's organization and also happens to be his nephew. When Big Al got arrested, Francesco thought he would be the one to step up and run the organization. Instead, Big Al kept calling shots and had Lorenzo step up to oversee daily operations. Francesco didn't see eye to eye on his uncle's decision-making, including the decision to bring Don into the family business.

Francesco held up Don's driver's license, shaking his head in disgust. "Look at this shit," he said to the other members of the Italian mob gathered around him. "This is who my uncle wants us to work with?"

"That man got money, though," one of the men muttered as he flicked through a pile of bank statements. This information was pulled on Don when Big Al had him looked up.

"Money ain't everything," Francesco snapped back, tossing the license onto the table. "He ain't one of us. He doesn't belong here."

The tension in the room was thicker than the haze from their cigarettes as the men continued rifling through Don's possessions. Some of them had worked for Big Al for years and didn't take kindly to an outsider like Don infiltrating their ranks, especially not a black man.

"Yo, Francesco, check this out," another man called from across the room. He held up Don's phone which kept ringing incessantly. The screen displayed numerous missed calls and unread text messages. "Seems like someone really wants to get ahold of our boy here."

Francesco grabbed the phone and scowled at the screen. The constant buzzing was grating on his nerves, but it also fueled his growing concern. "Whoever they are, we need to shut them down before they blow our cover. Letting outsiders in family business never turns out well. We don't even know where he came from."

"Or maybe we just need to get rid of him," one of the men suggested, a malicious glint in his eyes. "Without your uncle knowing, of course."

Francesco considered the idea, his mind racing with thoughts of betrayal. As much as he hated the idea of working with someone like Don, crossing his uncle was no small feat. But if they could pull it off, it would be a power move; one that would solidify his position at the top of the organization.

"Y'all really think we can do this without Big Al finding out?" another man asked, his voice thick with uncertainty.

"Without a doubt," Francesco replied confidently. "We just have to be smart about it. Nobody is going to know a thing."

As the men continued to plot against Don, the dark cloud of betrayal hung heavy over their heads. They knew the risks they were taking, but their desire for power and control outweighed their loyalty to Big Al. And in the grimy world, they inhabited, that was all that mattered.

Orlando sat in the corner of the room; his eyes fixated on Don's belongings sprawled across the table. The heavy scent of cigarette smoke hung in the air as he brooded over the rumors he'd heard. They said Don had been getting close to Isabella, and it burned him up inside. That woman was supposed to be his, not some outsider's interest.

"Man, y'all heard about that monkey and Isabella, right?" Orlando blurted out, unable to keep his jealousy contained. "I heard that they've been getting real cozy lately. She keeps popping up at that house they put him in."

"Who the fuck is Isabella?" one of the men asked.

"Ain't that Big Al's girl?" one of the other men chimed in, his voice thick with an Italian accent.

"Hell no," Francesco roared. "My uncle doesn't entertain the help. She's like a jeweler or something."

"Man, she ain't nobody's girl but her own," Orlando snapped, clenching his fist. "But if I had it my way, she'd be mine. I can't stand the thought of her with that monkey."

"Stay focused, we need to find something incriminating on this guy," Francesco ordered as he picked up Don's phone again, his fingers scrolling through messages and photos. The others followed suit, rummaging through Don's laptop that was taken from his condo back in Atlanta.

Orlando couldn't help but let his thoughts drift back to Isabella, her raven hair flowing down her back, the coy smile she wore when she looked at him. He knew he had to get rid of Don, not just for the power struggle, but for her heart. He needed her to see him as the man she should be with.

"I'm not finding anything on this dude," one of the men muttered, tossing paperwork onto the table. "It's like he's not even dirty. He seems legit."

"Keep looking," Francesco growled, frustration etched on his face. "We got to find something we can use against him."

"Man, you think Big Al is going to be cool with us digging through this shit like this?" Orlando asked, feigning concern. If anything, he wanted to fuel the fire and make sure everyone was on board to take down Don.

"My uncle ain't going to know," Francesco replied, his voice low and dangerous. "This is about protecting our organization and my family. We don't need an outsider coming in and messing things up."

As the men continued their search, Orlando's thoughts were consumed by Isabella and the prospect of finally claiming her as his own. All they had to do was find a way to take Don out of the picture, and everything would fall into place.

"Yo, check this out," one of the men called out, pointing to a screen in the security office they had just entered. On the live feed, they could see the lavish house and the crystal-clear pool shimmering under the sun.

"Damn, that's some nice digs," Orlando muttered, narrowing his eyes at the sight before them. Through the haze of envy, he spotted Lorenzo standing beside Don and Isabella. His heart raced at the sight of her, making him even more determined to remove Don from the equation.

"Look at them, all cozy and shit," Francesco sneered, clenching his fists. "We need to deal with this situation real quick before it gets out of hand."

"Definitely," Orlando agreed, the wheels turning in his mind. "I got an idea. We use a sniper to take him out clean from a distance. No mess, no fuss, and we don't have to worry about getting our hands dirty."

"Orlando, you are a cold cat, but I like it," Francesco said, nodding in approval. "It's quiet and efficient. That's how we do things."

"It's not going to work," Mattia muttered. He was a younger guy but put in a lot of muscle work for Lorenzo, including going to Atlanta to pick up Don. Your uncle and Lorenzo will immediately know it was us."

"No, they won't," Orlando replied, his thoughts focused on Isabella and the life they could have together once Don was gone. "All we have to do is find a good spot, set up, and wait for the right moment. Ain't no way Big Al will know it was us."

"Yes, he will," Mattia rebutted. "We have to make this shit look random. Like a robbery or something on the street. Maybe do a little home invasion. Kill him and then steal some shit to make it look authentic."

"Alright, let's get it done," Francesco commanded, his eyes flickering with determination. "I want this taken care of as soon as possible. The sooner we get rid of him, the better."

As the men filed out of the security office, their minds filled with dark intentions, Orlando couldn't help but smile to himself. Every step they took brought him closer to achieving his goals, and he knew that soon, everything would be as he desired. The only thing standing in his way was Don, and soon, he'd be nothing more than a distant memory.

Roman hesitated, the weight of betrayal feeling like an anchor around his heart. The others could smell blood in the water, but he was torn. He'd always been loyal to Big Al, and the thought of going against him made his stomach churn. As he watched Orlando's grin grow wider, something inside Roman snapped.

"Yo, hold up a minute," Roman interjected, his voice as firm as steel. "We need to think this through. We don't know what Big Al got planned for Don. Maybe there's a reason he has him around."

"Man, you are crazy," Francesco scoffed, dismissing Roman's concerns with a wave of his hand. "My uncle ain't here right now, and we have to do what's best for us."

"Come on, Roman, we ain't got time for this," Orlando added, the impatience clear in his voice. "The longer we wait, the more chance there is that Don finds out about our plans."

Roman clenched his fists, frustration boiling beneath the surface. He knew what they were doing was wrong, but it seemed like no one else cared. They were so blinded by their hatred and jealousy of Don that they couldn't see the bigger picture.

"Look, I get y'all don't like that guy being here," Roman said, trying to reason with them. "But this ain't just about us. This is about the whole organization. If we go behind Big Al's back and kill Don, who's to say we won't be next on the chopping block?"

"Roman, you soft, man," Orlando sneered, crossing his arms over his chest. "That nigger ain't one of us. He ain't never gonna be either. And if we don't take him out, he'll be taking our spots, laying up with our women, and running things while Big Al rots in prison."

"Enough!" Francesco barked, silencing everyone in the hallway. The tension was thick enough to cut with a knife, but Roman refused to back down. "Roman, I understand your loyalty to my uncle, but we have to take care of this ourselves."

"Francesco, you know I'd do anything for the family," Roman replied, his gaze steady and unwavering. "But I can't go along with this plan. It ain't right, and it's going to bring nothing but trouble."

"Fine," Francesco spat, glaring at Roman. "If you don't want to be a part of this, then stay out of our way. But when everything falls apart, don't come crying to us."

"Whatever, man," Roman muttered, feeling the eyes of his former allies burning into him as they left out. He knew he'd made enemies today, but he couldn't shake the feeling that betraying Big Al would lead them all down a path from which there was no return.

As the door slammed shut behind them, Roman took a deep breath, steeling himself for the consequences of his decision. He could only hope that somehow, he'd managed to make the right choice in a world where every move seemed like a mistake just waiting to happen.

*****

The shadows of the night cloaked the warehouse, as Francesco paced back and forth like a caged tiger, his face contorted with frustration. "We don't got time for this shit," he growled, clenching his fists. "Don's making moves, and we need to act fast before he sinks his teeth into our organization."

"Francesco's right," Orlando chimed in, his eyes darting around the room, still burning with jealousy over Don's rumored relationship with Isabella. "We can't afford to wait any longer. We let him get too close, and there won't be no turning back."

The men nodded in agreement, their faces tense and determined. Roman's refusal to participate only fueled their resolve, making them eager to prove him wrong.

"Alright then," Francesco said, taking a deep breath. "Let's do this. We hit Don tonight. Quick and clean. No loose ends."

The air crackled with anticipation as they began gathering weapons from hidden caches throughout the warehouse - sleek handguns, menacing shotguns, and wickedly sharp knives glistened under the dim lighting. The cold metal felt heavy in their hands, a solemn reminder of the gravity of their decision.

"Hey, I got a spot scoped out," Orlando announced, his voice low and urgent. "A rooftop across the street from Don's place. Perfect line of sight for a sniper shot."

"Good," Francesco replied, nodding approvingly. "Make sure you got an escape route planned out. We can't afford any slip-ups on this one."

"Already got it covered," Orlando assured him, a sly grin spreading across his face. "We'll be ghosts before anyone knows what went down."

"We can send someone in to take care of business and if that nigger runs out the house, we'll deal with him."

As the men loaded their weapons, checking and rechecking every detail, their thoughts raced with equal parts excitement and fear. For many of them, this was the first time they'd stepped so boldly outside of Big Al's orders, and the weight of their betrayal hung heavy in the air.

"Remember," Francesco said, his voice icy and resolute, "this stays between us. No one else needs to know what we're doing. You keep your mouths shut, and we'll come out of this on top."

With a final, shared glance, the men braced themselves for the impending attack, their hearts pounding in their chests like war drums. As they slipped out into the night, each man knew that there was no turning back - the die had been cast, and only fate could determine how this dangerous game would play out.

The tension in the building crackled like static electricity as the men went about their grim preparations. Mattia's fingers trembled slightly as he loaded the ammunition into his weapon, a cold sweat forming on the back of his neck. His thoughts raced, consumed by the weight of what they were about to do.

"Yo, Francesco," he started, trying to keep his voice steady. "We sure about this? I mean, Big Al ain't going to be happy if he finds out."

"My uncle isn't going to find out about this until tomorrow and he won't think that we were involved," Francesco snapped, his voice dripping with impatience. "This is for the good of the family, Matt. You think Don's going to stay loyal when he gets enough power? He'll take us all down, one by one. This is our chance to stop that from happening."

Mattia couldn't shake the gnawing feeling in his gut, but he knew better than to argue further. Instead, he tried to focus on the task at hand, forcing himself to remember that this was for the survival of the organization.

"Alright," Orlando chimed in, his voice high with excitement. "The sniper position is all set up. We ready to roll?"

"Let's do it," Francesco confirmed, his face a mask of determination.

The men filed out of the building, leaving the discarded remnants of Don's belongings scattered across the floor like the aftermath of a hurricane. They drove to their destination and were ready to strike. As they made their way to their positions, Mattia's mind swirled with doubt and fear. He stared at the ground as he walked, careful not to meet the eyes of the others - he couldn't let them see how conflicted he was.

"Yo, Mattia," Orlando called out, his voice low and conspiratorial. "You good, man? You look like you've seen a ghost or something."

"Y-yeah," Mattia stammered, forcing a tight-lipped smile. "I'm good. Just...just thinking about how this all going to go down, you know?"

"Man, don't worry 'bout it," Orlando replied with a dismissive wave of his hand. "We got this in the bag. He ain't gonna know what hit him."

As they approached their positions, Mattia couldn't help but glance up at the moonlit sky, silently praying for some kind of divine intervention to save them from the path they'd chosen. But the heavens remained silent, and the night air was heavy with foreboding. Orlando darted across the street, in order to secure his spot.

"Positions, everyone," Francesco ordered, his voice cold and distant. "It's time."

With a nod, Orlando settled into his sniper position, his finger hovering over the trigger as he took aim. The others took up their assigned roles, their faces set with grim resolve.

"I'm ready," Orlando whispered into a small walkie talkie, his voice barely audible over the pounding of his heart.

"Ready," came the collective reply, each man bracing themselves for the chaos that would inevitably follow.

Mattia closed his eyes for a moment, trying to block out the noise of his own ragged breaths. This was it - their point of no return.

Chapter 4

Don stood on the sidewalk, his eyes scanning the bustling street before him. The city's heartbeat thrummed beneath his feet; he could practically smell the opportunity in the air. Pulling out his phone, he dialed the number of the local dealership associated with Big Al. He would need a new ride to get around town and scope out commercial properties for his next venture.

"Yo, this is Don," he said into the phone, his voice low and smooth. "Lorenzo gave me this number to call for a car."

"Good morning, Mr. King. We've been expecting your call."

"I checked out the cars on your website. I would like to pick up that black 2023 Mercedes-Benz S-Class if is still available." There was a brief pause on the other end before the voice confirmed the time and date.

"Bet," Don replied before hanging up. He pocketed his phone just as Roman approached, the 6'2", 250-pound enforcer casting an imposing shadow over him.

"Lorenzo sent me," Roman said, his shaved head gleaming in the sunlight as he eyed Don with a mix of curiosity and respect. His muscular frame filled out the black leather jacket and jeans he wore, making him look every bit the tough guy he was. "I heard you're looking for a car, so you can go check out some property."

"That's right," Don replied, sizing up the man before him. He wasn't one to trust easily, but if Roman had been sent by Lorenzo, then that was good enough for now. "I also called the dealership dude and picked out a car. He told me it might be ready this evening."

"No problem. Word is, you've been through some shit, man," Roman said, his dark eyes sympathetic. "Big Al's got his hands full tryna keep his empire running from behind bars. It can't be easy for you either, being caught up in all this mess."

"Appreciate the concern," Don responded, keeping his tone neutral. "But I can handle myself. Right now, I gotta focus on findin' the right spots for his business."

"True," Roman agreed, nodding thoughtfully. "I can help you with that. I know the streets better than anyone else."

"Good," Don said, a hint of a smile playing at the corners of his mouth. "Then let's get to work."

As they walked towards the car, Roman provided Don with valuable insight into the internal power struggle within Big Al's criminal empire. He spoke of the factions and their leaders, the shifting allegiances, and the constant fight for control that threatened to tear them all apart.

"Big Al ain't going to give up without a fight," Roman assured him. "He's got people on the inside and out here working for him. But there are others who want to take his place. It's a dog-eat-dog world, man."

Don listened intently, his eyes sharp as he took in every detail, every nuance of Roman's words. This was information he could use – knowledge that might just keep him alive in the ruthless game he'd found himself in.

The sleek white Chevrolet Silverado cruised down the asphalt jungle, like a predator on the hunt for prey. Don sat in the passenger seat, tense but ready; his eyes scanning the streets as Roman navigated the city. The truck's engine rumbled like a sleeping beast, a low growl that seemed to echo through the gritty neighborhood.

"Man, I gotta tell ya," Roman began, his voice thick with turmoil. "This whole situation got me twisted up inside. On one hand, I got loyalty to Big Al. He took me in when I was just a street punk and gave me purpose, ya know? But then there's his nephew, Francesco... and I ain't gonna lie, he got some solid ideas for the organization."

Don listened attentively, nodding every now and then as he weighed Roman's words. He knew this was crucial intel on the power dynamics at play in Big Al's criminal empire.

"Francesco ain't no dummy," Roman continued, gripping the steering wheel tighter. "He got the brains and the muscle behind him. But sometimes, man, I wonder if he got the heart." Roman thought about the failed hit last night on Don. He heard it was Francesco and Orlando who called it off and sent everyone back home when they got spooked by a few cars that kept riding through the neighborhood.

"Is that so?" Don asked, his tone carefully measured. He'd had his suspicions about the organization from the start, and this information only served to confirm them.

"Yeah," Roman agreed, a dark cloud of doubt hovering over his expression. "He's a good kid, he's just a little stubborn when it comes to associating with outsiders. But we ain't all like that. Some of us still got Big Al's back, even if we ain't sure which way is up anymore."

"Appreciate the honesty," Don replied, making a mental note of Roman's allegiance. "Just remember – ain't nothin' set in stone in this game. Things change fast, and you gotta adapt or get left behind."

"That's so true," Roman said, nodding. "I'm just trying to navigate this mess, same as you."

As they continued their drive, Roman delved deeper into the inner workings of Big Al's criminal empire. He spoke of the various factions vying for control, their leaders and motivations, and the fragile alliances that threatened to shatter at any moment.

"Big Al got some loyal soldiers still, but there's a whole lotta snakes in the grass too," Roman explained, his eyes narrowing as he navigated a tight corner. "You gotta watch your back out here, Don. Trust no one but yourself."

"Believe me," Don replied, his gaze never leaving the grimy streets outside the car window. "I learned that lesson a long time ago."

"Hey, Don," Roman said, pulling the car into a small parking lot. "This spot right here got the best Italian food in Newark. Let's grab some grub while we wait for them to call about your car."

"Sounds good to me," Don replied, his stomach growling in agreement.

They walked into the dimly lit establishment, its worn wooden floors creaking under their weight. The smell of garlic and tomato sauce permeated the air, instantly transporting Don to memories of his mother's home-cooked meals. They settled into a booth in the back, away from prying eyes.

"Man, this place takes me back," Don mused, scanning the menu as an older waiter approached with glasses of water.

"Feels like home, don't it?" Roman agreed, catching the waiter's attention. "Two specials and a bottle of red, my man."

As the waiter shuffled off, Roman leaned in closer to Don. "Look, Don, I gotta level with you. You have to be very careful while you are here in Jersey." He lowered his voice, concern etched on his face.

Don smirked, taking a sip of his water. "Appreciate the heads up, Roman. But I been through hell and back. Ain't nobody takin' me out without a fight."

"Still, watch your back. Trust me," Roman insisted, his expression serious.

The waiter returned with their wine, expertly pouring them each a glass before disappearing back into the shadows. The two men clinked glasses, sipping their drinks as they let the tension dissipate for a moment.

"Real talk tho," Don continued, swirling the wine in his glass. "You ever thought about gettin' outta this life? Start fresh?"

"Shit, it ain't a day that goes by that I don't think about it," Roman admitted, his gaze distant. "But it ain't that easy. Once you in, you in for life. Ain't no walking away."

"Maybe," Don conceded, his thoughts drifting to his own desire for a better life. "But sometimes you gotta take a leap of faith. Can't keep playin' both sides forever."

"True," Roman said, raising his glass again. "To one day leaving the game."

"Leavin' the game," Don echoed, their glasses clinking together once more.

As they savored their meal and conversation, Don couldn't help but feel the weight of the impending danger bearing down on him. He knew things were about to get ugly, but he was prepared for whatever came his way – or so he thought.

After finishing their lunch, Roman led Don out of the restaurant and back onto the streets of Newark. The sun had climbed higher in the sky, casting a harsh light on the concrete jungle around them. They walked side by side, the tension from earlier having dissipated for the time being. Roman gave him a quick tour of the neighborhood they were in and the connection he had with each business in the area.

"Car should be ready now," Roman said, checking his watch.

"Good. Need to get movin' on this property search," Don replied, his mind already racing ahead to potential business opportunities.

They arrived at the dealership, an unassuming building with gleaming luxury cars parked out front. Roman escorted Don inside, where they were greeted by a wiry man in a crisp suit – the owner, no doubt.

"Ah, Mr. King, right on time," the owner said, extending a hand. "Your car is all set."

"Thanks, man," Don replied, shaking his hand. He then nodded towards Roman.

"He's also looking for some commercial properties in the area. You got any leads?" Roman asked the man.

"Of course, always happy to help out a friend of Alphonso's," the owner said, giving Don a calculating once-over. "What exactly are you looking for?"

"Somethin' with potential," Don answered, his eyes flicking to the showroom floor, where his new black Mercedes-Benz S-Class sat, gleaming like a predator. "I'm a real estate guru, so I'll know it when I see it."

"Understood," the owner said, nodding. "I'll have my assistant gather some information for you and send it your way."

"Appreciate it," Don said, offering a tight smile.

With the car keys now in hand, Don slid into the driver's seat, feeling the luxurious leather embrace him. The seat hugged him like a lover. Roman hopped back in his truck, and they pulled out of the dealership and onto the busy street.

As they cruised through Newark, the pair examined potential properties, discussing their merits and drawbacks. Roman offered his local knowledge of the area, which proved invaluable to Don's search. Don aimlessly drove around, looking for a hidden gem. After about an hour or so, he began following Roman as he led him through commercial areas he was familiar with.

"See that spot over there?" Roman asked, pointing to a run-down warehouse. "Used to be a hotspot for us. Been empty for a while now."

"Got potential," Don mused, taking in the building's size and location. "Could turn it into somethin' big."

"Definitely," Roman agreed. "Just watch your back. A lot of shady cats lurk around these parts."

"Always do, my man," Don replied, a steely edge to his voice.

Throughout the day, they visited various locations, with Don's mind whirring as he assessed each one. In his head, he was already mapping out plans, visualizing how he could use his real estate prowess to turn these dilapidated buildings into thriving businesses.

"Last stop," Roman announced as they pulled up outside an old factory.

"Shit, this place is huge," Don muttered, his eyes widening at the sight of the sprawling complex.

"Owned by a dude who owed Big Al big time. He ain't around no more," Roman explained, watching Don's reaction closely.

"Re. Let's check it out," Don said, his curiosity piqued.

After thoroughly inspecting the property, Don knew he had found the perfect project – a diamond in the rough, just waiting to be polished. As they climbed back into their vehicles, he couldn't help but feel a renewed sense of purpose, even with the danger lurking in the shadows.

Don pulled up to Roman's truck. "Appreciate you showin' me around," Don said, sincerity in his voice. "You've been a big help."

"Anytime, man," Roman replied, his gaze fixed on the property still. "Just remember what I said earlier about watching your back."

"I ain't forgettin'," Don assured him, his thoughts already shifting to the challenges that lay ahead. "I've survived this long for a reason."

"I feel you," Roman agreed, his tone somber. "Just be careful, yeah?"

"I will be," Don promised, as they pulled out of the lot and drove their separate ways, both men acutely aware of the battles that would soon come their way.

The night was thick with a stillness that hung heavy in the air as Don returned to his temporary residence, exhaustion creeping into every fiber of his body. He kicked off his shoes and peeled off his jacket, tossing it carelessly over the back of a nearby chair. His mind whirred with thoughts of the day's events and the potential commercial properties he'd scoped out. He undressed and then hopped straight into the bed. The weight of Roman's warnings pressed down on him, but for now, all he wanted was some sleep.

Don was knocked out. Between the jet lag, property searching and his extracurricular activities with Isabella, he had finally been able to get a good night's sleep. The cool breeze blew through a cracked window as the wind whistled through the night sky. The doorknob of the front door slowly turned, before the door creaked open. Don had no clue as the large home suffocated the sound within the halls.

A dark figure stepped into the home, being cautious of their footsteps. They peered around each corner, ensuring they wouldn't be detected. As they inched closer to the master bedroom, there was an eerie silence in the home. Stepping in, a smile spread across their face. Don laid in bed, unbeknownst to him there was a visitor hovering over him.

The fatigue of the week had caught up to him so much that he couldn't feel the presence of someone in his home. Luckily for Don, Isabella just wanted to spend a little more quality time with him. She stood at the foot of the bed, only wearing a trench coat and heels. A part of her hoped that Don would have been awake for some reason and would be able to remove her outer garment for her but instead, she silently slipped it off herself.

Isabella was now naked and slid underneath the covers. She pulled Don's arm over her body, allowing herself to get comfortable. Isabella was hooked. Big Al brought her into this operation because of her knowledge of gems and jewelry but he made it clear that she couldn't let business mix with pleasure. When she laid eyes on Don, she couldn't help but cross that line. She figured that since he wasn't part of the mob, her obsession was harmless.

Isabella tried her best to cherish the moment that she and Don shared but she wanted more. She solidified her decision when she got caught by Lorenzo and nothing negative came of it. Instead, she was able to have a front-row seat next to Don in the restaurant. That moment made Isabella feel powerful and she craved more of that power.

She stared at Don, mesmerized by his handsomeness. the moonlight bounced off his brown skin. She traced her finger around the edge of his beard, before leaning in for a kiss. Still, he didn't wake up. Even as he slept, Don had Isabella lusting over him in the worst way. Her hand slowly drifted from his beard down his bare chest. Isabella moaned as she felt her clit throbbing for attention.

With one hand on his chest, she used her other to address her burning desire. With two fingers, she toyed with her clit, sending pleasure through her entire body. "Don," Isabella moaned loudly, waking him from his sleep. Once his eyes opened, the sight of Isabella playing with herself sent him over the edge.

"What you doing here?" he asked in a groggy voice.

She responded by moaning his name louder.

"Damn. You are so fuckin' sexy," he said before grabbing her neck and pulling her on top of him. Isabella smirked before she planted a kiss on his lips. She eased her way down his waistline, gently unbuttoning his pants. With a gentle tug, Isabella freed Don's throbbing dick from its cage. She wrapped her hands around Don's shaft and began to stroke it slowly.

Isabella savored the moan that escaped his lips. She leaned down and began to kiss his shaft, causing him to throw his head back in ecstasy. Don wasn't going to stand for it. He grabbed her hair and pushed her head down onto his shaft. She began to take it deeper down her throat, making it plunge as far as it could go. She only stopped when she felt as if she was going to puke. She pulled herself away from his manhood, letting his dick pop out of her mouth.

As he laid in bed, Isabella straddled his waist. She leaned over him and forced his dick to her pussy lips. She began to sink down on his shaft, moaning as he penetrated her. Don grabbed her hips as she gyrated her hips back and forth. Isabella leaned forward, forcing Don to suck on her breasts. He thrusted his pelvis upwards, making his cock go deeper into her tight pussy. She moaned as his fingers dug deeper into her sides. She felt her body begin to shutter, announcing that she was about to climax. It was a good thing that Don had such a strong grip on her. When he felt his balls tighten, Don began to thrust his hips up and down at a fast pace.

"Yes," Isabella screamed in unison with his thrusts. They both moaned in unison until they climaxed at the same time. They both withdrew from orgasmic bliss, before lying next to each other in bed.

"This was a pleasant surprise," Don said, smiling from ear to ear.

"Be honest," Isabella whispered. "You think I'm crazy, don't you?"

"Naw." Don chuckled. "Maybe a little bit, but I like it."

"You like it?"

Don looked her up and down, looking like he wanted to devour her. "Hell yeah."

"What if I want you to love it?"

"Well, make me love it."

The two leaned in for another kiss, when they were interrupted by the sound of the front door being kicked in. Don hopped up from the bed and grabbed his gun which was on the nightstand. "Get under the bed," he ordered Isabella, as he prepared to investigate the loud noise.

As soon as he exited the bedroom, two masked men opened fire. Bullets whizzed by Don's head, and he ducked back into his room to avoid getting hit. His ears rang from the gunshots as he caught his breath and tried to calm down. Once his heartbeat slowed a bit, he took a few deep breaths and crouched next to his bed. The gun was heavy in his hand and the barrel shook with each shot. The men ordered Don to come into the hallway, but he had other plans. Don fired his weapon through the wall, in the direction of the front door. He could tell one of the intruders had been hit by a bullet because of how their voice changed tone as they were yelling. Gunfire continued flying as the intruders continued their attack.

Don’s heart rate was elevated and he felt the adrenaline pumping through his body. He looked at Isabella, who was lying flat under the bed, trying to keep as low as possible. If he had to die, he wanted to ensure that she remained unharmed. The gunshots had stopped around the same time as a door slamming shut. The men had taken cover.

Don ran through the house as fast as he could, ending up in the kitchen. He could hear one of the intruders running through the dining room. His life flashed before his eyes as he stood in the dark dining room, waiting for his attacker to come closer. Once the man crossed into the kitchen, Don pulled the trigger. He heard the scream of the intruder as a burst of blood hit the wall behind him. The intruder fell onto the floor. The sound of his body hitting the floor echoed throughout the house.

I gotta get back to Isabella, he thought as he hurried back to the bedroom. Don quickly searched for the other intruder. He popped his head in each room, hoping the second attacker would show themselves.

Don spotted blood smeared outside one of the hall bathrooms. He kept his gun aimed at the bathroom as he slowly crept up to the door. He didn't hear any sounds coming from inside. "Announce yourself and I'll let you live," Don yelled.

There was silence. "I said announce yourself motherfucka," Don ordered.

"Okay," a voice said. "Just don't shoot. I'm already hit and I need to get to a hospital."

"Drop your fuckin gun on the ground and slowly open the door."

"Okay. Promise me you won't shoot when I open the door."

"I promise. Just open the fuckin' door."

Don listened as the intruder's footsteps came closer to the bathroom door.

"Okay, I'm opening the door now. Please don't shoot me," the voice said.

The door slowly opened and the intruder stepped out into the hall. "I'm sorr-"

Don let two shots rip from the gun before the intruder could finish his statement. The shots ripped into the man's chest, dropping him instantly.

With both intruders dead, Don's breathing slowed as he tried to process what had just happened. His heart hammered in his chest, a mix of fear and adrenaline coursing through his veins. He returned to the bedroom to check on his lover. Isabella cowered in the corner, her eyes wide with terror.

"Are you okay?" Don asked, his voice laced with concern as he lowered the gun.

"Y-yeah, I'm fine," she stammered, tears streaming down her face.

Don exited the bedroom and approached the motionless bodies, his mind racing. Who were these men? And why had they come for him? He yanked the ski masks off their faces, revealing their true identities. Italian, no doubt about it – from their olive skin to their thick, dark hair.

"Motherfucka," Don muttered under his breath, rage bubbling up inside him once more. The pieces were starting to fall into place, and Don knew he couldn't ignore the truth any longer. This wasn't some random attack; it was a message, a warning from someone within Big Al's empire. Someone who wanted him dead.

"Who are they?" Isabella whispered, her voice trembling. She stood at a distance, not wanting to get a look at death up close.

"Enemies," Don replied tersely, clenching his jaw. He stared at the lifeless faces, committing their features to memory. This was far from over, and he would make damn sure he found out who was responsible for this attempt on his life – and make them pay.

But for now, he needed to keep Isabella safe and focus on the task at hand. He had a job to do, and he wouldn't let anyone – not even Big Al himself – stand in his way.

Don paced through the dimly lit living room, his heart pounding hard against his chest. His thoughts were a whirlwind of paranoia and suspicion. *Who had sent those hitmen? Why now?*

"Big Al must've set this shit up," he muttered to himself, clenching his fists. "That's the only way they could've gotten to me."

"Are you sure?" Isabella asked, her voice shaky. She stood in the corner, her eyes darting nervously around the room. "Why would he do that?"

"Cuz I ain't just some pawn in his game no more," Don growled. "I'm makin' moves, gettin' my own territory, and plannin' to set my family up for life. He must see that as a threat."

Images of Big Al's cold, calculating eyes played over and over in Don's mind. Had he truly been part of the plan to take him out? And if so, who else was involved?

"Isabella," Don said, turning to face her. "You gotta tell me – and be straight with me – did you have anything to do with this? Did Big Al ask you to get close to me or somethin'?"

"Wh-what? No!" she stammered, tears welling up in her eyes. "I swear, Don. I didn't know nothing about this."

Don watched her closely, searching for any sign of deceit. But all he saw was genuine fear and confusion. He wanted to trust her, but the nagging doubt still lingered.

"Alright, alright," he sighed, rubbing his temples. "We can't stay here, though. We gotta move, to make sure we're not sittin' ducks. And I need to find out who's behind this; who in Big Al's crew is tryna take me down."

"Okay, let's go," Isabella whispered, grabbing her jacket. As they prepared to leave, Don couldn't help but feel the weight of the looming conflict within Big Al's criminal empire.

"Listen," he said, his voice low and serious. "We gotta watch our backs now more than ever. There's gonna be a war brewin' over this shit. Big Al ain't gonna be happy when he finds out I survived, and whoever's behind this will come after me again."

Isabella nodded solemnly, her eyes filled with determination. "I'm with you, Don. Whatever it takes."

"Good," Don replied, gripping his gun tightly as they headed for the door. He knew that the road ahead would be paved with danger and betrayal, and that he would have to navigate a world where even those closest to him could become his enemies. But he was ready for the fight – and he wouldn't rest until he uncovered the truth and brought those responsible to justice.

Don's heart pounded in his chest as he and Isabella made their way through the darkened streets of Newark. The cold air bit at his face, but it did little to numb the storm of emotions raging within him. He clenched his jaw, his mind racing with thoughts of betrayal and vengeance.

"Where we going, Don?" Isabella asked, her voice barely above a whisper.

"Somewhere safe," he replied tersely, his eyes darting back and forth, scanning for potential threats. "We'll go to your spot. Just give me the directions."

"Okay," she nodded, her breath visible in the frosty night air. Isabella instructed Don on how to get to her apartment.

As they moved deeper into the shadows, Don couldn't shake the feeling that he was being watched. The hairs on the back of his neck stood on end, and a cold sweat began to bead on his brow.

"Yo, you see that?" he muttered, stopping abruptly and turning his head around. "I think that car back there is following us."

"What car?" Isabella whispered, gripping Don's arm tightly.

"This one right here!" he hissed, holding his gun up, ready to defend himself. A moment later, a car drives by their vehicle, and Don felt a mix of relief and frustration wash over him. The paranoia was getting to him, making him believe things that weren't happening.

"Must of been my imagination," he muttered, running a hand through his hair. "Come on, let's keep movin'."

They continued on, the city's grit and grime seeming to seep into Don's very soul. With every passing moment, he felt the weight of his situation pressing down on him, like a vice tightening around his skull. He didn't know who he could trust anymore – not even Isabella.

"Listen," he said suddenly, his voice strained. "I gotta ask you again. Were you in on this shit? Did you know they were comin' for me?"

"What — Don, no!" Isabella exclaimed, her eyes wide with shock. "I swear, I didn't know nothing about this! You gotta believe me."

Don stared into her eyes, searching for any hint of deception. All he saw was fear and hurt – the same emotions that welled within him.

"Alright," he said finally, his voice cracking. "I believe you... for now."

As they reached the safety of Isabella's apartment, he could feel the walls closing in around him. The paranoia gnawed at his sanity like a starving rat, and he knew that he would have to confront the demons within Big Al's criminal empire sooner rather than later.

But for now, he would rest – and prepare for the trials that lay ahead. With a deep, shuddering breath, he locked the door behind them, sealing himself off from the treacherous world outside.

"Get some sleep, Isabella," he muttered, collapsing onto the floor. "Tomorrow, we go to war."

Her soft sobs echoed through the room as sleep eluded Don, his mind consumed by the chaos of his shattered life. He knew he would need all his strength and cunningness to survive the storm that was brewing, but the turmoil within him threatened to tear him apart before he even had the chance to fight back.

Chapter 5

The stench of death hung heavy in the air, a metallic tang that clung to the back of Don's throat. He stood in the once-pristine living room, now a bloody battleground, surrounded by the lifeless bodies of two Italian hitmen. The sight of them sprawled on the plush carpet, their faces frozen in expressions of shock and betrayal, only fueled his paranoia. He'd been played, and now he was exposed - left vulnerable in the heart of enemy territory.

Don paced across the room, eyes darting from window to door, expecting another traitor to pop out at any moment. His jaw clenched, sweat beading on his forehead as his hand gripped the cold steel of the gun tucked into his waistband. No one could be trusted anymore, not in this twisted game of deception.

The sudden sound of a car pulling up outside sent Don's heart pounding against his chest. He pressed himself against the wall beside the front door, gun drawn and ready for whatever came next. In his mind, he reeled through all the possibilities - another ambush, perhaps, or an impossible visit from Big Al himself.

"Hey, Don! It's Lorenzo!" The familiar Italian accent rang through the otherwise silent house, and Don's grip on his weapon tightened. As much as he wanted to believe in Lorenzo, the man could have always been a snake, ready to strike at the first opportunity.

"Come on in," Don called out, voice steady despite the adrenaline coursing through his veins. He'd have to play it cool, keep Lorenzo talking, and hope that he could get some answers before things went sideways.

Lorenzo entered, the door creaking on its hinges as it swung open to reveal the well-dressed mobster. He took one step inside, eyes flickering over the grisly scene laid out before him, before fixing his gaze on Don. "I heard about the attack. Are you okay?"

"Does it look like I'm okay?" Don snapped, his paranoia bubbling dangerously beneath the surface. He didn't give a damn about politeness anymore; all he wanted was the truth.

Lorenzo's eyes widened in horror as they scanned the blood-splattered walls and the lifeless bodies of two of his men, propped up in the living room like discarded ragdolls. "Holy shit, Don! What happened here?" He stammered, his voice quivering with disbelief.

"Shut up!" Don snarled, his paranoia reaching a boiling point. Without thinking, he leveled his gun at Lorenzo's chest, his finger twitching on the trigger. "You better give me a damn good reason not to blow you away right now!"

"Whoa, whoa!" Lorenzo raised his hands defensively, his face a twisted mask of worry and uncertainty. "I didn't have anything to do with this! I swear on my children!"

Don's mind raced, his thoughts an unrelenting storm of anger and suspicion. Could he trust Lorenzo? The man was slicker than black ice on a cold Atlanta night, but Don had to admit that the raw shock in Lorenzo's eyes looked genuine.

"Look, Don," Lorenzo continued, desperation creeping into his voice. "I just came around to check on you after hearing about the attack from Isabella. I didn't know it was gonna be...like this." He gestured helplessly at the carnage surrounding them.

"Keep talkin'," Don growled, his gun still trained on Lorenzo's chest. He could feel his heart pounding, a wild drumbeat echoing through his veins.

"Man, if I was behind this, you think I'd walk in here like this? With no backup or nothing?" Lorenzo's words tumbled out, rapid-fire and earnest. "I'm not stupid, Don. I know you'd put a bullet in me before I could even blink."

"Damn straight," Don replied, though some of the tension in his shoulders began to ease. He didn't want to believe that Lorenzo was involved, but in this world of cutthroat gangsters and backstabbing hustlers, trust was a currency he could ill-afford. But for now, it seemed like Lorenzo was telling the truth.

"Alright," Don muttered, lowering his gun slightly but keeping it at the ready. "But if I find out you had anythin' to do with this...you're a dead man, Lorenzo. You hear me?"

"Crystal clear, man," Lorenzo nodded fervently, relief washing over his face as the cold steel of Don's gun moved away from his chest. "I'm never going to cross you. I can promise you that."

As they stood there, surrounded by the remnants of violence and treachery, Don couldn't help but wonder who he could really trust in this unforgiving game. And more importantly, how long would it be before the walls came crashing down around him?

"So, what exactly happened here?" Lorenzo asked, scanning the carnage that littered the room. His eyes were wide with confusion and alarm.

"I was laid up with Isabella and they kicked the door in. They started shooting, trynna take me out," Don growled, his grip on the gun unwavering. "And I'm gonna find out who sent them. Do you know who they are?"

Lorenzo looked at them with disappointment. "The one on the left is Orlando and the other one is Mattia."

Don took a step back, his eyes staring down the sights of the gun. "So, they are your people."

Lorenzo let out a deep sigh. "Yes. Yes, they are. They run under Francesco but they did not have any authorization to carry out an attack on you."

Don furrowed his brow, trying to make sense of Lorenzo's explanation. "Francesco? What does he have to do with this?"

"He's been trying to take over the organization, Don. He's been making moves behind Big Al's back," Lorenzo explained, his voice low and cautious. "I tried to warn Big Al that this was going to happen, but he wouldn't listen."

"This is bullshit," Don snapped, the bitter taste of betrayal stinging his tongue. He narrowed his eyes at Lorenzo. "I need to talk to Big Al. Now."

"Alright, alright," Lorenzo said, raising his hands in a placating gesture. He pulled out his phone and dialed Big Al's number. "I'll get him on the line for you."

As Lorenzo waited for the call to connect, Don's mind raced with possibilities, each one more treacherous than the last. Who was truly behind this? And how deep did this conspiracy go?

"Hey, Big Al, you there?" Lorenzo asked into the phone, his voice strained with urgency. But there was no response. The silence on the other end felt heavier than the tension in the room. "Big Al?"

"Put it on speaker," Don demanded, his finger still hovering over the trigger. He needed to hear everything.

"Big Al, come on, man. Pick up!" Lorenzo shouted again, but still, nothing. The silence was deafening, and Don's heart pounded in his chest like the beat of a thousand drums.

"Damn it," Lorenzo muttered, ending the call. "He didn't pick up, Don. I don't know what's going on, man."

"Neither do I," Don replied, the ice in his voice barely masking the storm of emotions roiling beneath the surface. "But I'm gonna find out. And when I do, there'll be hell to pay."

"Whatever you need," Lorenzo said, his eyes filled with genuine concern. "I got your back."

"Let's just hope that's enough," Don murmured, finally lowering the gun but keeping it close at hand. In this deadly game of cat and mouse, he knew he couldn't afford to let his guard down for even a second.

Don's eyes narrowed as he studied Lorenzo, his mind racing with suspicion. The silence from Big Al weighed heavily on him, feeding his paranoia. Could it be that the man he'd once shared a cell with, the one he thought he could trust, had betrayed him?

"Somethin' ain't right," Don muttered, clenching his jaw and tightly gripping the gun. His instincts were screaming at him to stay vigilant, to prepare for what might come next.

"Chill, man," Lorenzo said, trying to ease the tension in the room. "The boss is going to call back. He got to."

"Does he?" Don snapped, his voice dripping with doubt. As much as he wanted to believe in Big Al, the unanswered call gnawed at him, threatening to unravel the last threads of trust holding them together.

"Look, I don't know what you think is going on, but—"

Lorenzo's words were cut off by the shrill ring of his phone. Both men jumped, their gazes locked on the device as if it held the key to their survival.

"Answer it," Don commanded, his tone cold and unyielding. Lorenzo hesitated for a moment before obeying.

"Big Al?" he asked hesitantly, his eyes darting between the phone and Don.

"Put it on speaker," Don demanded, refusing to risk any secrets being kept from him.

"Y'all need to relax," Big Al's voice boomed through the small speaker, the sound filling the room like an invisible presence. "Now, tell me what the hell is going on over there and why I got all of these missed calls from you at this time of the morning."

"Al," Don began, his voice heavy with fear and anger, "I've been set up. Two of your men are dead, and someone's trynna take me out too. I don't know who to trust anymore. I'm cut off from my family, my friends... my whole damn life."

"Jesus Christ," Big Al muttered, the shock evident in his voice. "I didn't know anything about this, Don. I swear on my life."

"Then who's behind it?" Don demanded, his fingers twitching as he fought the urge to unleash his frustration on something - or someone.

"Look, we'll figure it out," Big Al reassured him, his voice firm and steady. "For now, you have to lay low and keep your head down. Lorenzo, stick with him. Y'all watch each other's backs, you hear me?"

"Got it," Lorenzo nodded, though his eyes held a tinge of uncertainty.

"Hell naw," Don sighed, taking a deep breath as he processed the weight of the situation. "I don't need none of your people with me. I don't trust any of them."

He knew that trust was a luxury he could no longer afford, and survival would depend on his ability to navigate the treacherous waters ahead. But for now, he had no choice but to rely on those around him, however uneasy it made him feel.

"Al, I'm tellin' you, man. Your people took everythin' - my phone, my wallet, my ID. I ain't got nothin'," Don said, his voice strained from the weight of the situation.

"I can't believe this," Big Al muttered, disbelief evident in his tone. "I didn't know about any of this, Don. I promise you that." There was a brief pause before he barked at Lorenzo, "Give him back his stuff. Now!"

Lorenzo hesitated for a moment but quickly complied, fetching Don's belongings from his car and placing them into his outstretched hand. Francesco and his men had left the items scattered on the floor in a warehouse, but one of their men had returned the items to Lorenzo. As Don pocketed his wallet and phone, a renewed sense of determination flickered within him. He couldn't afford to waste any more time - he needed to get out of there and find some answers.

"Thanks, Al," Don grunted, nodding to Lorenzo as he turned to leave. "I'll be in touch when I figure out what's goin' on here."

"Be careful, Don," Big Al warned, his concern genuine. "I don't like the sound of all this. Something ain't right."

"Trust me, I know," Don replied grimly, stepping out into the unknown. The chilly air bit at his skin, sending shivers down his spine as he hurried to his car. His heart raced with each step, paranoia nipping at his heels.

Meanwhile, Big Al's fury bubbled to the surface as he tore into Lorenzo over the phone. "How the hell did you let this happen? You're supposed to have control over everything that's going on!"

"Boss, I swear, I didn't know about any of this," Lorenzo stammered, desperation creeping into his voice. "I'll fix it though. I'll find out who's behind it, and we'll make 'em pay."

"You better," Big Al growled, his warning laced with a thinly veiled threat. "Or it'll be your head."

As Don drove away from his once-safe haven, the adrenaline coursing through his veins left him feeling both wired and exhausted. He couldn't shake the nagging suspicion that someone close to him had betrayed him, but who? And why?

"Damn," he muttered to himself, gripping the steering wheel tightly as he navigated the dark streets. "Can't trust nobody no more."

Determined to stay one step ahead of the danger lurking in the shadows, Don continued driving into the heart of the city, searching for a temporary refuge where he could begin to untangle the web of lies and deceit that had ensnared him. Meanwhile, Lorenzo had to face the consequences of his lack of control over their organization.

"Who were the men who attacked Don?" Big Al demanded over the phone, his voice was cold and commanding. "I want to know right now or you'll be answering to me."

"It was Orlando and Mattia," Lorenzo said, his voice strained as he tried to maintain control of the situation. "They came out of nowhere with this shit. I didn't expect them to turn on us like that."

"Orlando and Mattia?" Big Al repeated, his tone incredulous. "Those two have been with me since the beginning. I basically raised those boys. They know better than to cross me."

"Well, they did," Lorenzo replied, a hint of frustration creeping into his voice. "And now we have to deal with the mess they made. They had to be under the orders of Francesco."

"Don't worry about that," Big Al said firmly. "I'll take care of my nephew myself. But first, we need to focus on

Don. He's in danger, and we need to make sure that nothing happens to him."

"Agreed," Lorenzo said, relief washing over him as he realized Big Al wasn't blaming him for the situation. "I'll get the guys on it right away."

"Good," Big Al said, his voice resolute. "I'm counting on you to keep our new asset safe. If something happens to him, we can kiss our future goodbye. His people will want answers and it will create problems that none of us need right now.

"I'll do my best," Lorenzo promised, his determination echoing through the phone. "We'll get to the bottom of this, boss. I swear it."

"Your word better be enough." The threat in Big Al's voice was unmistakable, sending a chill down Lorenzo's spine.

Lorenzo watched as Don's car vanished around a corner. He quickly jumped into his own vehicle, determined to follow and protect Don, while also hunting for answers to satisfy Big Al's thirst for retribution.

As he drove, Lorenzo couldn't help but feel a sense of foreboding, a gnawing unease that clung to him like a second skin. This day had already taken a deadly turn, and he knew that there were more twists and turns yet to come.

Don's phone buzzed in the center console, shattering the tense silence that had enveloped the car. He snatched it up, his heart pounding as he answered the call. "Yeah?"

"Hey, Don, it's Roman," came the voice on the other end. "I heard about what went down at your place, man. That shit ain't right."

Don clenched his jaw, his grip on the steering wheel tightening even further. "You got any idea who did this, Roman?"

"Look, I know you probably think it was Big Al, but it wasn't him. Trust me."

"Trust you?" Don spat out, his skepticism dripping from each word. "How the hell am I supposed to trust anybody after last night?"

"I'm telling you, man – Big Al didn't have anything to do with it," Roman insisted, his voice firm and steady. "But we don't got time for all that right now. You need to know something else."

"What's that?" Don asked warily, his eyes darting between the road ahead and the rearview mirror.

"Word on the street is you got someone tailing you," Roman revealed. "Lorenzo, I think. Can't say for sure, but you better watch your back."

"Shit," Don muttered, the realization hitting him like a ton of bricks. His mind raced, trying to process the fact that one of Big Al's top bosses could be following him. Was this another setup? A trap?

"Listen, Don, I got you," Roman assured him. "I'm gonna help you shake him off your tail. Just follow my directions, alright?"

"Alright, let's do this," Don agreed, adrenaline coursing through his veins as he prepared to outmaneuver his pursuer.

"First, make a right at the next intersection you see," Roman instructed. "Then gun it for two blocks and hang another right into that first alley you spot. Keep going straight 'til you hit the other side and that should put you on a one-way street going in the opposite direction from wherever Lorenzo is coming from."

Don followed Roman's directions to the letter, his tires screeching as he whipped around corners and sped through the shadowy alleyways. His heart hammered in his chest, every nerve in his body on high alert. The weight of betrayal and the threat of danger hung heavy in the air, mixing with the scent of exhaust fumes and fear.

"Where to now?" Don panted, his breath coming in short, ragged gasps as he emerged from the alley onto a deserted street.

"Head toward a highway," Roman said. "Once you're there, get on and book it. You should be able to lose him if you keep switching lanes and moving fast. Lorenzo won't be able to keep up with all of that."

"Got it," Don replied, his voice tight with determination. The roar of the engine filled the streets as he merged onto the highway, weaving between cars like a madman, his eyes constantly scanning the rearview mirror for any sign of Lorenzo.

"Stay sharp, Don," Roman warned. "Lorenzo ain't no amateur – he ain't gonna give up easy."

"I know," Don responded, steeling himself for whatever might come next. "But neither am I."

With each passing mile, the chances of losing Lorenzo grew slimmer, but Don refused to give up. He was a survivor, a man who had clawed his way out of the darkest depths and risen above the chaos time and time again. And he'd be damned if he let anyone take him down without a fight.

Don's heart raced as he sped down the highway, finally feeling the distance grow between him and Lorenzo. The adrenaline pumping through his veins began to subside, but confusion clouded his mind like a thick fog. He knew he couldn't keep driving aimlessly – he needed a place to lay low and figure out his next move.

"Roman," Don said into the phone, his voice hoarse from the persistent tension, "I need a spot to crash for the night. Somewhere safe, off the radar."

"I got you," Roman replied, the sound of keyboard clicks filling the brief silence. "There's a bunch of hotels in Atlantic City which is about two hours from your current location. It's like a little Vegas over there with a bunch of casinos and shit. Nobody will be able to find you out there."

"Appreciate it," Don murmured, his thoughts heavy with betrayal and uncertainty. Who could he trust, if not those he'd considered new business partners? And what kind of enemy had slithered its way into the shadows of his life, waiting for the perfect moment to strike?

As he cruised down the highway, Don finally made it to Atlantic City. He pulled into the parking lot of the busy hotel, then second-guessed being around so many people. Don surveyed his surroundings with a wary eye. He took to the streets to find another spot that better fit his needs.

Don went a few miles away from the hustle and bustle or the casino properties and spotted a shabby motel. A dimly lit neon sign flickered above the entrance, casting an eerie glow on the cracked pavement beneath it. Shadows danced across the walls, the wind whispering secrets through the rustling leaves.

"Remember, Don," Roman's voice echoed in his head, "trust no one right now. You got to stay sharp if you want to make it out of this alive."

Don clenched his jaw, determination settling deep within him. He would get through this, no matter what it took. But first, he needed some rest – a chance to clear his head and gather his strength.

"Come on," he muttered to himself, stepping out of his car and making his way to the motel office. "One night. Just one night, and then I'll figure this shit out."

As Don stood at the motel's front door, he knew that this wouldn't be an easy path. He had been thrust into a dangerous game where the stakes were higher than ever before, and there was no telling who would make it out alive. But there was one thing he could count on – his own resilience, honed through years of hardship and adversity.

"Bring it on," he whispered into the night, steeling himself for whatever lay ahead.

Chapter 6

The Royal Inn Motel stood like a decaying relic of the past; its once vibrant neon sign now flickering pitifully in the dim light of the Jersey evening. The cracked and chipped paint on the walls only served to showcase the motel's age, while the rusty bars on the windows seemed more like an invitation for trouble rather than a deterrent. It was the kind of place where shadows lurked around every corner, and the stench of desperation clung to the air.

Inside, the questionable cleanliness of the linoleum floor matched the dinginess of the stained walls. The burnt-orange bedspread, decorated with cigarette burns and suspicious stains, did little to comfort those who sought refuge within the motel's confines. Amidst this squalor, Don paced nervously, his dark eyes scanning the room as if expecting trouble to burst through the door at any moment.

The shrill ring of Don's phone pierced the heavy silence, jolting him from his thoughts. His heart pounded in his chest as he glanced at the screen, noting yet another unknown number. He clenched his jaw, sweat beading on his brow as anger and apprehension battled within him. The repeated calls were no coincidence – they were a deliberate reminder that his enemies were closing in, eager to draw first blood and settle scores.

"Damn," Don muttered under his breath, ignoring the call and tossing the phone onto the bed. He knew answering could jeopardize everything he had built, but the weight of the unresolved conflict gnawed at him relentlessly. The safety of his friends and loved ones was on the line, and that knowledge sent a shiver down Don's spine unlike any icy breeze outside ever could.

For now, Don forced the anxiety to the back of his mind, focusing on the task at hand. He needed to stay sharp, to keep his wits about him in this treacherous environment. The Royal Inn Motel was far from a sanctuary, but it would have to suffice as Don plotted his next move in this deadly game of survival.

With a deep breath, Don stepped out of the motel room, his eyes scanning the dimly lit parking lot. He knew he couldn't afford to waste any more time – every second spent in this place put him at greater risk. His boots crunched on the gravel beneath him as he strode purposefully towards his car, the cool air biting at his exposed skin.

"Time to get down to business," he muttered, his breath fogging up in the frosty air.

Reaching the trunk, Don fumbled with the keys before finally unlocking it with a soft click. He flung the lid open, revealing an assortment of hurriedly packed bags, including one that contained the diamonds and cash. The urgency in his movements was palpable as he hastily retrieved a duffel bag and slung it over his shoulder.

"Don! Is that you?" a familiar voice called out, stopping him in his tracks.

Don's heart skipped a beat as he turned to face the source of the voice. There she stood, her tall frame silhouetted against the amber glow of a flickering streetlight. Ayanna, the woman who had wormed her way into his heart and then shattered it into a million pieces, now stood before him like a ghost from his past.

Ayanna ran into his arms, squeezing him tighter than she had ever done in the past. Don didn't know how to respond, so he wrapped his arm around her and completed the embrace. He was also confused as to why she was in New Jersey and how she found him. "What the hell are you doing here?" he softly asked, emotions getting the best of him.

"I thought you were dead," she replied with tears running down her cheeks.

Don's heart sank as he realized the depth of Ayanna's pain. He had left without a word, disappearing without a trace, and leaving everyone to believe that he was gone forever. And now, here she was, standing before him with tears streaming down her face.

"I'm sorry," Don whispered, his eyes locked onto hers. "I had to get away for a while. It wasn't safe for me to stay home at the time."

Ayanna's grip on him tightened, her face buried in the crook of his neck. "I was so worried about you," she sobbed.

Don held her, his mind racing as he tried to figure out how to explain everything to her. He knew that he couldn't stay here for long – the danger was too great, and he couldn't afford to be caught off guard. But he couldn't bear to leave Ayanna like this, not when she needed him the most.

"Listen," he said, pulling away from her and gently holding her at arm's length. "We need to go inside. It's not safe for either of us to be out here."

Ayanna's eyes widened in fear. "What do you mean it's not safe?"

Don hesitated, trying to choose his next words carefully. "I've been involved in something...dangerous. Something that could get us both killed if I don't handle it correctly. So, we need to get inside right now."

Ayanna's face paled at his words, and Don knew that he had to act quickly. He grabbed her hand and beelined for his room. Don locked the door and stared out the windows, ensuring that no one was following either of them or trying to ambush him again.

He looked back at the former love of his life, torn between his lingering feelings for Ayanna and the harsh reality of the life he now lived. As the cool wind whipped under the door, he knew he had to figure out the true reason for Ayanna's sudden appearance.

"How did you find me?" Don asked.

Ayanna was initially hesitant to answer the question. She knew her methods of tracking Don down were improper, seeing as though she was no longer a police officer. "Your phone," she muttered. "I had the phone company put a ping on it. It was off for a while, but a couple of days ago it was turned on and that's when I started getting the updates that your phone was in Jersey.

Cop shit, Don thought. His eyes widened as he took in the sight of Ayanna, a mixture of anger, pain, and shock coursing through his veins. He clenched his fists at his sides, struggling to process her sudden appearance. The love he had once felt for her came rushing back like a tidal wave, crashing into the walls he had built around his heart.

"I was worried sick about you. But now that I found you, I need to know why you're here."

"None of your damn business," he spat, his jaw tightening. Despite his anger towards Ayanna, he couldn't ignore the way his pulse raced at the mere sight of her.

"Look...I know we got history, but I'm just trynna make sure you're safe, Don. That's all," she insisted, her eyes pleading with him to open up. "After everything that went down in Atlanta, I gotta know you ain't in over your head."

"Over my head?" Don scoffed, his tone dripping with contempt. "Seems like it's you who's always a step behind. I can handle myself just fine."

He turned away from her, attempting to mask the conflicting emotions raging within him. Memories of their life together tore at him, a stark reminder of what they had lost. As much as he hated to admit it, seeing her reignited the ember of hope that still flickered deep inside him.

"Please, Don," Ayanna begged, her voice barely more than a whisper. "I can tell you're in trouble. What are you mixed up in?"

"Listen, woman," Don said, his voice low and dangerous. "I ain't got time for this. I got my own business to handle, so just stay the hell out of it."

"Can't do that, Don," Ayanna replied, her eyes narrowing with determination. "You were always there for me when I needed you, and now you're in danger. You think I'm gonna just walk away from that?"

"Stay out of this shit," he warned, his voice cracking as he fought to keep his emotions in check. "You made your choice a long time ago. It ain't nothin' left for you here."

"Maybe...maybe we can still help each other," she suggested hesitantly, her eyes searching his for any sign of hope. "We were a good team once, Don. Maybe we could be that again."

"Things ain't that simple no more," he said, his voice heavy with sorrow. "There's too much bad blood between us now. This ain't our fight no more."

"Maybe," she conceded, her eyes downcast. "But either way, I ain't leavin' you, Don. Not this time."

As she stood resolute before him, Don was once again reminded of the strength and loyalty that had drawn him to Ayanna in the first place. And while he knew their past was marred by betrayal and heartache, he couldn't deny the flicker of hope that still burned within him.

Don hesitated, his mind racing as he tried to find the right words. He knew Ayanna deserved answers, but there was still a gnawing doubt in the pit of his stomach. She was a cop once, and her allegiance to her profession could create problems for Don and his operation.

"Look," Don began cautiously, trying to keep his voice steady. "I ain't gonna lie to you, but I... I can't give you all the details. It's bigger than just me, it's about protectin' the people I care about. I can't have a cop knowing what's going on here."

"I'm not a cop anymore," Ayanna admitted. "They fired me."

"Fired you? For what."

"For falling in love with you and jeopardizing the case they had."

"Are you serious?"

Ayanna studied his face for a moment before nodding slowly. She could see the worry etched in Don's features, the weight of responsibility that he carried with him every day. It was that same sense of loyalty that had once drawn her to him, and while she recognized that things were different now, she couldn't help but feel a renewed connection to him.

"I still can't tell you why I'm here. You don't need to be wrapped up in none of my bullshit."

"Fine," she relented, her tone softening. "But I need to tell you something, Don. Something important."

"Go ahead," he said, bracing himself for whatever bombshell she was about to drop.

"Ramir's dead," Ayanna blurted out, her eyes filling with tears. "He got killed a couple weeks back. And everyone thought you were dead too 'cause you went missing."

Don's heart dropped like a stone in his chest. Ramir, his right-hand man, his brother in arms, and Ace's little cousin. Dead. A flood of memories washed over him – late nights scheming about how to grow the business, the adrenaline-fueled heists they'd pulled together, the shared laughter and pain. Don's knees buckled as he fell back into the wall. The news was unexpected and was too much to bear. The realization that he would never see Ramir again hit him like a sucker punch to the gut.

"Damn," he muttered, his eyes clouded with grief. "Ramir... He was a good kid. He didn't deserve to be killed."

"Nobody knows who did it, Don," Ayanna continued, her voice cracking. "His body was dismembered. They found his remains at the club you got for Cash."

"Are you fuckin' serious?" Don asked, his eyes beginning to water. "Who the fuck would do that type of shit?"

"They don't know, but everyone thought something may have happened to you too because you weren't answering your phone and your condo was empty. I know your family is worried sick about you. But I know ya'll won't rest until ya'll find out who did this to Ramir. And when you do, I wanna be there. I wanna help you get justice for Ramir."

"You don't need to be involved in this mess," Don insisted, his voice tight with emotion. "You got your own life now, your own problems. You don't need me draggin' you back into this shit."

"Maybe not," she admitted, wiping away the tears that had betrayed her. "But I can't just stand by and watch you fight this battle alone, Don. I still love you."

For a long moment, Don stared at Ayanna, seeing the fierce determination shining through her eyes. Though he knew their past was complicated, the bond they shared ran deep, and he couldn't deny that having her by his side would make him feel stronger.

"Alright," he finally conceded, his voice barely more than a whisper. "But we gotta be on the same page. No more secrets, no more lies, and definitely no cop shit."

"Deal," she agreed, a small smile flickering across her face for the first time since their reunion.

As Don prepared to respond, his phone rang loudly, cutting through the tense atmosphere. He glanced at the screen and saw a New Jersey number lighting up the display. Anxiety twisted in his gut as he hesitated to answer, knowing that the conversation could send him spiraling deeper into an already dangerous situation.

"Hey, Donny boy," Big Al's gravelly voice boomed through the line, his tone a mix of enthusiasm and false cheeriness. "Glad you picked up. Been trying to reach you all afternoon since our earlier conversation. I'm sorry about the attack on your life. I promise, whoever did that is gonna pay big time."

Don clenched his jaw, trying to control his emotions as he stared out the motel room window. Ayanna watched him closely, concern etched on her face. "Yeah, well, it ain't nothin' I can't handle, Al," he replied tersely, his anger bubbling just below the surface.

"Good to hear, good to hear," Big Al continued, oblivious to Don's growing frustration. "Listen, man, we still got business to discuss. I still need your help with these diamonds – we gotta legitimize 'em, ya know? And once we do, the empire's gonna expand like you wouldn't believe."

Don shifted uncomfortably, his loyalty to his friends and family warring with his obligation to Big Al. The pain of Ramir's death was still fresh, and the thought of diving back into the criminal underworld left a bitter taste in his mouth. But he couldn't deny the allure of power and wealth that Big Al dangled in front of him.

"Al, I don't know," Don began hesitantly, his eyes darting to Ayanna, who seemed to sense his internal struggle. "I got some personal stuff goin' on right now, and I ain't sure if I can just drop everything to help you with this."

"Come on, Don," Big Al cajoled, his voice taking on a more insistent edge. "You know we always looked out for each other. Besides, what's more important than loyalty and family? You help me with this, and I'll make sure you're taken care of – no more worrying about constantly watching your back."

Don sighed, feeling the weight of the decision pressing down on him. He glanced over at Ayanna once more, her eyes pleading with him to choose a different path. But as much as he wanted to walk away from it all, he knew that Big Al's offer was too tempting to pass up.

"Okay," he finally conceded, his voice heavy with resignation. "I'll think about it. But if I do this, we're even. Understand?"

"Of course, my man!" Big Al replied cheerfully, clearly satisfied with Don's answer. "You won't regret this, Donny boy. Trust me."

As Don was about to end the call, he couldn't shake the feeling that he had just made a deal with the devil himself. And as he looked into Ayanna's tearful eyes, he knew that his loyalty had just put everyone he cared about at risk.

"Look, Al," Don said with a hint of frustration in his voice. "I got real problems right now. I was just informed that one of my people was killed back in Atlanta. I need to focus on avengin' his death and protectin' my people back home."

"Wait, wait, wait," Big Al replied, his voice dripping with incredulity. "You're choosing to go back to the risks in Atlanta rather than making millions here with me?"

Don clenched his jaw, knowing that what he was asking might be considered a betrayal by some. But this was about more than loyalty; it was about keeping everyone he cared about safe.

"Al, I ain't sayin' it's gonna be easy," Don admitted, his voice softening slightly. "But sometimes you got to make sacrifices for the greater good. You got a chance to clean up your act, legitimize these diamonds, and give your family a better life. The longer I stay here, I'm not sure I'll have a family to go back to."

Big Al's face was a mixture of anger and hurt as he considered Don's words. His eyes narrowed, and his lips pressed into a thin line, trying to suppress the emotions that threatened to bubble over.

"I hear you," Big Al acknowledged, his tone cold and calculated. "But you know, I got a lot invested in this operation, and I'm not just going to walk away from it all. We're family now, Don, and family sticks together no matter what. I need you here with me, helping me keep things running smooth."

"Al, I can't –" Don started to protest, but Big Al cut him off.

"Listen to me," he insisted, desperation creeping into his voice. "We can't just abandon everything we are building. I need your help to maintain control of this operation, to keep it from falling apart. You're the only one I trust, Don. The only one."

Don hesitated, torn between his loyalty to Big Al and his desire to protect those he left behind in Atlanta. He knew that staying in New Jersey would put all their lives at risk, but how could he turn his back on someone who had always been there for him?

"Fuck, I'll do it," he finally said, his voice heavy with the weight of his decision. "I'll stay, Al. But we gotta find a way to end this conflict. And we need to do it quick, before more people get hurt."

A smile crept onto Big Al's face as he heard Don's agreement. His tone changed to one of determination and triumph.

"Thank you, Don. We'll figure this out together, like we always do. Trust me, everything's going to be alright," Big Al said, his voice low and serious. "I got people all over the world who owe me favors. I can get you the manpower you need to handle this problem in Atlanta. Just say the word, and I'll make it happen."

"Al, you sure about this?" Don asked, his voice filled with doubt. "This ain't no small-time beef. If my suspicion is correct about who did this, it's gonna be a big problem to handle."

"Trust me," Big Al replied confidently. "I've been building connections for years. I can pull some strings and get you the resources you need to come out on top. We'll put an end to this mess once and for all. Your enemies in Atlanta won't know what hit them. I'll give you an army of my men that will handle any problem you have."

As Don listened to Big Al's promises, he couldn't shake the feeling that he was being pulled deeper into a web of danger. But knowing that he had Big Al's support gave him a sense of strength, a belief that he could overcome any obstacle.

"You got a deal," Don agreed, exhaling deeply. "Let's do this. Get your people ready. We gonna take care of business here and then take care of business down in Atlanta."

"Consider it done," Big Al replied, determination resonating in his voice.

As the conversation ended, Don couldn't help but feel a sense of apprehension settle over him. He knew that siding with Big Al meant putting his own people in danger, but he couldn't bring himself to abandon the man who had helped him through so much. No matter the cost, he would have to find a way to balance the demands of loyalty and survival.

Chapter 7

Don leaned against the kitchenette counter, sipping his lukewarm coffee as he watched Ayanna sleep on the couch. The sun was just beginning to rise, casting a soft glow through the window. He hadn't slept at all, his mind racing with thoughts of what he needed to do next.

Ayanna stirred, her eyes fluttering open as she looked up at Don. "Why ain't you sleep?" she asked groggily.

"Couldn't," Don replied, setting his coffee down and walking over to the couch. "We need to talk, Ayanna."

"About what?" she asked, pushing herself up into a sitting position.

"About Big Al's plan for me and how it could help us get outta the game and make some legit money," Don said, his voice serious and determined.

Ayanna frowned, concern etched on her face. "What you talkin' 'bout, Don?"

He tossed the small velvet sack to her. Ayanna picked it up and poured the contents from the sack into her hand.

"Wow," she muttered, marveling at the beautiful stones. "Where did you get these?"

"The Italians. One of them is worth two million."

"Two million dollars?"

"Yup."

"So, what do they want you to sell these or something? There's no way you won't raise red flags if you try to cash these in."

"Big Al got a plan to set up some jewelry stores. He wants me in on it to help him find the right spots for these shops." Don paused for a moment, gauging Ayanna's reaction. "This could be my ticket outta the drug game, Ayanna. A chance to live a clean life."

"Is that really possible, Don?" Ayanna asked hesitantly. "I mean, your family has been in this game so long..."

"Trust me," Don said, his eyes locked onto hers. "We can make this work. For us and our families."

Ayanna nodded slowly, her fear and concern giving way to cautious hope. "Alright, Don. Let's do it."

"Good," Don said, offering her a hand to help her up from the couch. "Now get dressed. I wanna take you somewhere."

"Where we going?" Ayanna asked as she stood up, stretching out her stiff limbs.

"Scoutin' for some potential spots for Big Al's jewelry stores," Don replied, a determined glint in his eye. "Time to start makin' moves."

As they drove through the streets of New Jersey, Don kept a close eye on Ayanna. Her brow was furrowed in thought, but she seemed to be warming up to the idea of their new venture. They cruised through a rundown neighborhood that had seen better days, its buildings crumbling and abandoned. This was where they would change their lives.

"See that spot over there?" Don pointed to an old building with boarded-up windows. "That could be it. It's got character, and with a little work, we could turn it into somethin' special. What you think?"

Ayanna studied the building, her eyes scanning its exterior, imagining what it could become. "Yeah," she said finally. "I can see it, Don. I can see you doing this."

"Yup," Don replied, a proud smile spreading across his face. "Now let's go make some things happen."

Ayanna stared at the rearview mirror, her fingers tapping a nervous rhythm on the armrest. "Don," she said, her voice laced with concern, "why ain't we headin' back to Atlanta? I thought that's where you were doing this legit business."

Don glanced over at Ayanna, his eyes momentarily leaving the road. "Trust me, baby girl," he replied, reaching over to squeeze her hand reassuringly. "It's all part of the plan."

"Plans change," she muttered, her gaze drifting back to the mirror. Her unease had settled deep in her chest, and she couldn't shake the feeling that something was off.

Just then, Don's phone rang, its shrill tone cutting through the silence. He frowned at the screen before answering. "Big Al, what's good?"

Ayanna listened as Don's conversation unfolded, her heart pounding in her ears. Big Al's gravelly voice was barely audible on the other end, but she caught snippets of their discussion.

"LLC for the transactions...legitimize the possession of the diamonds...keep our hands clean..."

Don nodded along with Big Al's words, his face a picture of focus and determination. "Yeah, I got you. We'll set it up right away."

He hung up the phone and turned to Ayanna, his expression softening. "Hey, listen..." he began, his voice gentle yet firm. "This thing we're doin' with Big Al, it's bigger than us. It's about settin' up our family for the future. We gotta lay low for a bit, get everything in place before we head back to the A. You feel me?"

Ayanna sighed, her shoulders sagging with the weight of her own conflicted thoughts. She knew Don was right, that this was The Street Kings chance to escape the drug game and build something real. But the unknowns, the danger that still lurked in the shadows, it was all too much.

"I guess," she whispered, her grip on the armrest tightening. "I trust you, Don. Just promise me one thing."

"Anything," he replied, his voice full of conviction.

"Promise me that at the end of the day, you'll make it out alive."

Don took a deep breath. "I promise."

The sun blazed down on the concrete jungle as Don drove through the city, his eyes darting from one building to the next in search of potential locations for more jewelry stores. The phone buzzed again, the words "Big Al" flashing across the screen. Ayanna tensed in her seat, still uneasy about their current situation.

"Big Al, what's good?" Don answered, his tone shifting to a more serious note.

"Listen, Don," Big Al began, his voice dripping with caution. "I'm not going to lie to you, man. I got reservations about doing business with my own people, especially Francesco. A few of those snakes have been plotting to take my spot. I wanted to reach out to one of them to find someone that can help make the businesses look legitimate, but my gut is telling me not to involve them in any of this."

Don gripped the steering wheel tighter, the tension in the car growing thick. "Yeah, I feel you. But we gotta move forward with this plan, right?"

"Absolutely," Big Al replied, determination seeping into his voice. "But that's why I need you, Don. You're not blood, you're not part of the mob, and that means you don't have a hidden agenda. We have an opportunity to clean this money, start legit businesses, and get out of the game for good. This is the end game."

"Man, I'm with you on that," Don said, his mind racing with thoughts of what his future could be. "We'll keep it tight, make sure everything runs smooth. You got my word."

"Good, good," Big Al responded, relief evident in his voice. "You take care now and watch your back. Especially around Francesco."

The call ended, leaving Don to stew in his thoughts. He glanced over at Ayanna, her expression a mix of worry and determination. She caught his eye, giving him a small nod of reassurance.

"Yo," Don began, his voice filled with resolve. "We're gonna make this work, you hear me? We're gonna walk away from this with somethin' real, somethin' we all can be proud of. And ain't nothin', and I mean nothin', gonna stand in our way."

Ayanna's hand found his on the steering wheel, her grip firm yet comforting. "I believe in you, Don," she whispered, her voice strong and unwavering. "Together, we'll build a better future for all of us and our families."

As they drove through the city, their eyes locked on the horizon, Don and Ayanna knew that the road ahead wouldn't be easy. But with each other by their side, they were ready to face whatever challenges awaited them, united in their pursuit of a better life.

The sun was setting over the Jersey skyline, casting a golden haze on the city. Don and Ayanna pulled up in front of a nondescript office building, the location

Lorenzo had chosen for their meeting. The streets were mostly empty, except for a few pedestrians walking by, oblivious to the significance of what was happening inside the drab structure.

"Ready for this?" Don asked, his voice steady as he looked at Ayanna.

"Let's get it done," she replied with determination, her eyes reflecting the fire burning within her.

As they entered the building, they found Lorenzo waiting for them in the lobby, his sharp suit contrasting against the worn-out interior of the place. Next to him stood Dominic Ricci, Big Al's lead criminal attorney, clutching a briefcase full of documents. A woman in her mid-forties, dressed in professional attire, completed the trio – she was the business attorney hired to ensure that everything went smoothly.

"Ah, there you are, my friend!" Lorenzo greeted Don, his Italian accent thick and welcoming. "I trust you're ready to proceed?"

"Damn right," Don replied, extending his hand to the attorneys. "Let's get this show on the road."

Lorenzo paused when he saw Ayanna, curiosity getting the best of him. "And who do we have here."

"Hello, I'm Ayanna. I'm Don's...umm..." she hesitated, not knowing what her place was in Don's life. "...girlfriend."

Lorenzo and Don shot each other glaring looks. Lorenzo wasn't aware that Don was seeing anyone, especially the way he was spending most of his time with Isabella. "Interesting. Nice to meet you."

They made their way to a small conference room, its walls adorned with faded certificates and generic paintings. It wasn't much to look at, but it would serve its purpose. As they sat around the table, the business attorney wasted no time in getting down to brass tacks.

"Alright," she began, opening her laptop and shuffling through her papers. "We'll start by creating a holding company and an LLC for the properties. Mr. Lorenzo, I understand that you and Mr. King have already selected a few suitable locations for the businesses?"

"Si, signora," Lorenzo confirmed, handing over a list of addresses. "All prime real estate, as per Don's request."

"Excellent." She turned to Don. "Now, I've been instructed to put everything in the name of someone that is not directly associated with either of the other organizations.

"That's correct," Don replied. He turned to Ayanna. "You want it in your name, or you want me to find someone else?"

Ayanna's heart was beating out of her chest. A part of her wanted to go along to help Don out, but another part was wondering what the hell she was getting herself into. She lived a life dedicated to protecting and serving and now she was about to lay in bed with two drug organizations. "You can put it in mine," she muttered.

"It will be in her name," Don replied.

The attorney looked at her and smirked. "Okay, ma'am. All I need now is your identification and for you to sign on this dotted line of this paperwork. That way, all income generated from the properties will be legally yours."

"Sounds good to me," Ayanna replied, her voice steady despite the weight of what they were about to do.

"Alright then." The business attorney handed Ayanna a pen. "I'll need you to sign here, here, and here."

Ayanna took a deep breath, knowing that with each stroke of the pen, she was helping to secure the futures of two of the country's biggest drug organizations. Don watched her intently, his heart swelling with pride at the woman he once loved taking control of her own destiny.

"Perfect," the attorney said as Ayanna finished signing. "Now, Mr. Ricci, please sign here as the managing member of the LLC."

As Dominic's pen touched the paper, Don couldn't help but feel a mix of excitement and trepidation coursing through him. This was it – they were on their way to legitimizing their operation, building a better life for themselves and their family. He knew there would be more challenges ahead, but he was ready to face them head-on.

"Congratulations," the business attorney said as she closed her laptop. "The paperwork is complete. You are now the proud owners of a new holding company and an LLC. I already received the startup funds for the businesses, so I will proceed with putting in bids for the properties on the list. I wish you all the best of luck in your new venture."

"Thank you," Don replied, shaking hands with her and Dominic Ricci. "We appreciate your help."

"Anytime, Don," Dominic said, giving him a nod. "Remember, we're always here if you need us."

With the meeting adjourned, Don, Ayanna, and Lorenzo exited the office building, stepping back into the fading light of day. As they looked out over the city they called home, one thing was clear: the game had changed, and they were ready to play by their own rules.

Don stepped into the street, his mind racing with strategies and connections he needed to make in order to secure the diamonds and strike back at the enemies of the Street Kings. He knew that to pull this off, he had to forge new alliances and hone his skills in the gritty underworld of crime and deception.

"Yo, Lorenzo," Don said, catching his attention as they walked towards their cars. "We gotta start buildin' a strong team to protect these businesses, man. Reach out to some old contacts, see who's still loyal to Big Al."

"I got you, Don. I know a few cats that might be down for this," Lorenzo replied, nodding in agreement.

As they continued talking, Don's mind was focused on the task ahead. He could already envision the intricate web of alliances, deals, and betrayals that would soon be set into motion. It was going to be a high-stakes game, and Don was determined to come out on top.

"Hey, hold up," Don said suddenly, stopping in his tracks and squinting at a figure lurking in the shadows across the street. "Ain't that Francesco?"

"Damn, you got eyes like a hawk," Lorenzo muttered, narrowing his own gaze on the man in question. "What's he doing here?"

"Let's find out," Don replied, striding purposefully towards Francesco, who seemed to be waiting for them to notice him.

"Ah, Don," Francesco greeted with an oily smile as Don approached. "I heard you were back in town. Can't say I'm surprised to find you here, signing papers and all that."

"Cut the crap, Francesco," Don snapped, not in the mood for pleasantries. "What do you want?"

"Can't a man offer his congratulations?" Francesco asked, feigning innocence. "I heard about your new venture with my uncle. I just wanted to make sure you're doing right by him, that's all."

"He doesn't have to answer to you," Lorenzo interjected, stepping up beside Don with a scowl.

"True," Francesco conceded, his eyes never leaving Don's. "But maybe you should consider putting everything in my name instead. You know, for safekeeping."

Don clenched his fists and fought to control his anger as he replied, "Big Al trusts me, and so does Lorenzo. You ain't gettin' shit from us."

"Fine," Francesco spat, his false smile dropping away. "Just remember, Don – I got eyes on you."

"Get lost," Don growled.

"Look, Don," Francesco said, leaning against the brick wall of the attorney's office. "I'm gonna be straight with you. My uncle's time is up. He's locked away for good, and I'm the one who's been keeping this organization afloat. I deserve to be in charge."

"Is that right?" Don asked, his voice dripping with sarcasm as he crossed his arms.

"Damn straight it is," Francesco replied, his eyes narrowing. "And when I take over, things are going to change around here. We don't need outsiders like you sticking their noses where they don't belong."

"Outsiders? You think just 'cause I ain't Italian, I ain't got what it takes to handle business?" Don challenged, his anger bubbling beneath the surface.

"Let me put it this way," Francesco sneered. "You head back to Atlanta, forget about all this jewelry store nonsense, and we'll call it even. You get to live your life, and I get my rightful place in the family. I'll handle everything here. I'll even take care of Isabella for you too."

Don stared at Francesco, taking in his arrogant posture and smug expression. He could see the greed and ambition behind his eyes, and he knew that Francesco would stop at nothing to secure his position. But Don had never been one to back down from a challenge, and he couldn't let Francesco win without a fight.

"Francesco," Don said slowly, his tone measured and ice-cold. "You really think you're the man for the job? You think you can just walk in and take over for Big Al, like it's nothin'? You must be outta your damn mind."

"Watch your mouth, boy," Francesco spat, the veneer of civility slipping away. "You don't know who you're messing with."

"Neither do you," Don retorted, his eyes locked on Francesco's. "Big Al trusts me, and I ain't gonna let him down. So, take your pathetic little offer and shove it."

"Suit yourself," Francesco sneered, pushing himself off the wall. "But remember this, Don – you just made a big mistake. You're gonna regret crossing me."

"Save your threats," Don snapped, his heart pounding in his chest as he watched Francesco stalk away. He knew that he had just made an enemy of one of the most dangerous men in Big Al's organization, but he couldn't back down now. He had to see this through, for Ayanna, for Big Al, and for himself.

"Man, you got balls standing up to him like that," Lorenzo remarked, clapping Don on the shoulder as they walked back to their cars.

"Got no choice," Don replied, his jaw set in determination. "We gotta stick together if we're gonna make this work."

"Damn right," Lorenzo agreed, getting in his vehicle and starting the engine. "Let's get out of here and show these fools what we're made of."

Francesco turned around. His face contorted into a twisted smile, revealing his true nature. "You know what, Don?" he yelled out. "I was the one who sent those men to kill you. And I'm going to send some more until the job is done."

A storm of rage surged through Don's veins, his muscles tensing as he clenched his fists. Francesco had no idea the fire he'd just ignited. Without another word, Don ran up on him, and swung his fist, smashing it into Francesco's smug face.

"Motherfucker!" Francesco roared, stumbling back from the force of the blow. Blood dripped from his split lip as he glared at Don with pure hatred burning in his eyes. He lunged forward, throwing a punch of his own.

Don barely managed to dodge the incoming blow, feeling the wind brush past his face as Francesco's fist narrowly missed him. They both traded punches, each man landing heavy hits on the other. The sound of fists colliding with flesh echoed through the air, mixing with their grunts and curses.

But the fight between Don and Francesco didn't go unnoticed. Francesco's men emerged from the shadows, guns drawn and aimed at Don. Their unwavering expressions made it clear they wouldn't hesitate to pull the trigger.

Just as Don felt the cold barrel of a gun against his temple, Lorenzo stepped up with his usual air of confidence, flanked by several armed men ready to defend their boss.

"Put them fucking guns down!" Lorenzo barked, his men leveling their weapons at Francesco's crew. "This ain't the time or place for this shit!"

The tense standoff continued for several heart-pounding seconds, neither side willing to back down. But eventually, with a begrudging nod from Francesco, his men lowered their weapons and retreated.

"Let's get out of here, Don," Lorenzo said, motioning for his men to follow suit. His voice strained as the distant wail of police sirens approached. "We got what we came for."

As they walked away from the scene, Don couldn't shake the feeling that this was only the beginning of a much larger battle. He knew he couldn't let his guard down now, not with enemies like Francesco lurking in the shadows. But for the moment, Don had made a powerful ally in Lorenzo, and together, they'd face whatever challenges awaited them head-on.

"Come on, Don," Ayanna said, tugging at his arm. "Let's get out of here." Her eyes held a mixture of fear and concern, her heart still racing from the near-death encounter.

"Right," Don muttered, casting a final glance at the retreating figures of Francesco and his men before turning to leave with Ayanna.

As they climbed into Don's car, the adrenaline began to dissipate, replaced by the weighty realization of what they'd accomplished. They had successfully set up the holding company and LLC, putting them both in Ayanna's name. It was the first major step toward legitimizing their operation and securing a future free from the drug game that had consumed their lives for so long.

"Baby, you did it," Ayanna breathed, her voice wavering with emotion as she looked over at Don. "You really did it."

"Yeah, we did," Don replied, allowing himself a small smile. He could see the pride shining in Ayanna's eyes, and it stirred something deep within him – feelings he thought he had buried long ago. But he couldn't focus on that now; there was still much work to be done.

"Let's head back to the motel," he suggested, starting the engine and pulling away from the curb. "We got a lot of planning to do."

As they drove through the city streets, the events of the day replaying in their minds, Don couldn't help but feel a sense of satisfaction. Despite the dangers that still loomed large, he had taken a crucial step toward building a better life for himself and those he cared about. It was a daunting task, but with Ayanna by his side and newfound allies like Lorenzo, he felt ready to face whatever challenges awaited.

"This all feels like a dream," Ayanna said softly, her hand resting on Don's thigh as they neared the motel. "Having our own legit business, and you being able to leave the streets behind."

"Hell yeah," Don replied, his voice thick with emotion. "It's finally happening."

"Thanks to you," Ayanna said, leaning in to plant a soft kiss on his cheek. "You always find a way to make things right, Don. I'm proud of you."

The warmth of her lips lingered on his skin, stirring feelings he hadn't allowed himself to acknowledge in weeks. But he knew he couldn't afford to let his guard down, not with so much at stake. He needed to stay focused, to keep pushing forward until their goals were achieved and their enemies vanquished.

"Let's celebrate when we get back," Ayanna suggested, her eyes sparkling with excitement. "Just us two, like old times."

"Sounds perfect," Don agreed, his heart swelling with a mixture of pride and anticipation. Tonight, they would revel in their accomplishments and allow themselves a brief escape from the treacherous world they inhabited. And tomorrow, they would rise to face whatever challenges awaited them, stronger and more determined than ever before.

The champagne flowed freely as Don and Ayanna toasted to their future, laughter, and warmth filling the dimly lit motel room. The amber glow of streetlights filtered through the curtains, casting a golden hue over the intimate scene. As they drank, their inhibitions loosened, and Ayanna found herself inching closer to Don, her body craving his touch.

"Remember all them nights we used to spend together?" she slurred, her fingers tracing idle patterns on his chest. "All those dreams we had?"

Don's heart raced at her touch, the memory of their past passion clouding his thoughts. He still loved Ayanna, but he couldn't deny the growing affection he felt for Isabella. Their connection ran deeper than business, and the thought of betraying her trust filled him with guilt.

"Y-yeah," he stammered, struggling to keep his voice steady. "But things ain't the same now, Ayanna. I want to be honest with you. I care about you so much, but I got feelings for someone else too."

Ayanna's eyes met his, her expression a mix of hurt and understanding. She knew Don better than anyone else and could sense the weight of his internal conflict. With a sigh, she withdrew her hand and leaned back against the headboard, giving them both some much-needed space.

"Isabella, right?" she asked, her voice low and heavy with resignation. "I heard that guy say her name earlier.

It's all good, Don. I ain't gonna force you into nothing you ain't ready for."

Don exhaled, relief washing over him at her acceptance. "I just need some time, ma," he said, reaching out to squeeze her hand reassuringly. "You know how it is."

Ayanna nodded, a wistful smile playing on her lips. "Yeah, I feel you," she replied. "We can just celebrate tonight, like old friends. And figure the rest out later."

"Sounds like a plan," Don agreed, his spirits lifting at the prospect of enjoying the rest of the night free from emotional turmoil. They clinked their champagne flutes together and continued to discuss their next steps for achieving their goals.

"Once we got these businesses set up, ain't nobody gonna be able to touch us," Ayanna mused, her eyes shining with ambition. "We'll be untouchable, and all that dirty money is gonna be clean."

"Exactly," Don replied, his determination renewed. "And once Big Al's diamonds are secured, we'll have enough capital to expand, to really make a name for ourselves in this city."

"With you by my side, I know we can make it happen," Ayanna declared, raising her glass in a final toast. She knew in the back of her mind that she was going to get her man back. "To our future, Don. To us."

"To us," he echoed, feeling the fire of ambition burning brighter than ever before. Together, they would conquer the streets of New Jersey, then Atlanta, and then forge a new path for themselves, leaving the darkness of their past far behind.

Chapter 8

As the sun crept over the horizon, casting long shadows in the dingy motel room, Don lay restless on the worn mattress. His mind raced with thoughts of Ramir's death and his dealings with the Italians. It felt like a heavy weight was crushing him, making it impossible to breathe. He clenched his fists, nails digging into his palms, as he tried to regain some semblance of control.

"Damn, I can't take this shit no more," Don muttered under his breath, tossing the threadbare blanket aside. He swung his legs off the bed, the cold linoleum floor chilling his feet. Standing up, he paced back and forth, the frustration and anxiety gnawing at him like a dog with a bone.

Yo, something's gotta give, he thought, stopping abruptly. He knew he needed to reach out to Cash, hoping that his cousin would have some answers or, at least, provide some comfort in these trying times. Grabbing his phone, he dialed Cash's number, but the call wouldn't connect. "Goddamn reception in this hellhole," he cursed, slamming the phone down on the cheap particleboard dresser.

Don tried to dial out with the motel phone, but no buttons lit up. The phone might as well have been a receiver and a mouthpiece, nothing more. He slammed it down in frustration and sat back down on the bed.

Desperate, Don knew he had to get creative. He searched the room for a piece of paper and a pen, finally locating both among the clutter. Scrawling a message on the paper, he folded it up and tucked it inside his pocket. Slipping on his jacket, he stepped out into the chilly New Jersey morning air, scanning the area for someone who could deliver the makeshift message to Cash.

"Hey, you!" Don called out, spotting a shifty-looking employee lingering near the entrance of the motel. The man eyed him warily, clearly sizing him up before responding.

"Yeah, whatchu want?" the man asked, stepping closer.

"Look, I don't have no service on my phone for some reason. I need you to call all of these numbers until somebody picks up. Whoever answers, give him the number to my room and tell him it's Don.

"Man, I ain't no damn messaging service," the man spat, glaring at Don with disdain.

"Listen, I ain't got time for this bullshit," Don snapped back, reaching into his pocket and pulling out a wad of cash. "You see this? This is just a taste of what you'll get if you do this for me. You in or not?"

The man's eyes widened at the sight of the money, greed momentarily overcoming his skepticism. He hesitated for a moment before snatching the paper from Don's hand. "A'ight, man. I'll make the call. But don't think you can come around here barking orders like you some big shot."

"Whatever. Just make sure you get in contact with one of them," Don replied, shoving the money into the man's hand before stalking back toward the motel room.

Don paced the dingy motel room, his nerves frayed and fists clenched. He stared at the broken motel phone on the nightstand, willing it to ring. The silence was suffocating, broken only by the distant hum of traffic outside. He took a deep breath, trying to steady himself before the call came through.

"Hello," he answered immediately.

"Yo, Don! It's about time you hit us up!" Nate's voice boomed through the speaker, relief evident in his tone.

"Man, you don't even know what I've been through," Don replied, sinking into a worn-out chair.

"Talk to me, man. What happened?" Nate asked, concern lacing his words.

"Long story short, I got mixed up with these Italians. Their boss is the one that helped get me out of jail, so I owed him a favor. They popped up at my spot and took me. The boss wants me to work for them, but his nephew tried to get me killed," Don explained, recounting the harrowing ordeal.

"Shit, Don. You gotta be more careful out there," Nate admonished him. "But I'm glad you're alright. We've been looking all over the city for you."

"Listen, I got more news," Don continued, glancing over at Ayanna who was knocked out on the couch. "Ayanna's with me," Don whispered.

"Wait, Ayanna? The cop bitch? Can you trust her?" Nate demanded, clearly taken aback.

"Yo, she ain't a cop no more," Don reassured him. "She risked everything to come out here and find me. She's also helping me wrap up things here with the Italians."

"If you trust her, I trust her," Nate conceded. "But we gotta be careful, Don. We can't afford any more surprises."

"Trust me, I know what I'm doing," Don said, his eyes locked on Ayanna with a determined expression.

"Good. 'Cause we got enough shit to deal with right now," Nate replied, his voice heavy with the weight of their shared burdens.

Don knew that Nate was right - they had to tread carefully and watch each other's backs if they were going to survive this war. And with Ayanna by his side, he felt a renewed sense of hope that they just might make it out alive.

"Yo, Nate, what's the word on Ramir's death?" Don asked, his voice cracking with emotion as he clenched his fists at his sides. "We gotta get back at those responsible."

"Man, we been puttin' in work trynna find out who did it," Nate replied, the anger evident in his voice. "Turns out it was Deuce and those Colombian fuckers. We're gonna make 'em pay for what they did to our boy."

"Damn straight," Don growled, his blood boiling at the thought of avenging Ramir. He glanced over at Ayanna, who was waking up.

"Only problem is, once this war's over, we might lose our connect," Nate added, his tone shifting to concern. "So, even if we knock him off, the streets are gonna dry up."

"Shit, we'll figure somethin' out. But first, we gotta handle these Colombians," Don insisted, his mind racing with plans and strategies for retaliation.

"True that," Nate agreed. "But what about you, man? When you comin' back to Atlanta?"

Don hesitated, staring at the floor as he contemplated his next move. "I don't know yet, fam. I got a lot going on up here."

"Look, Don, I get it. But Ramir's funeral is at the end of the week. You need to be there," Nate urged, his voice taking on an almost pleading tone. "Cash gonna be glad to see you."

"Fuck. I didn't think about the funeral. I promise I'll be there," Don finally said, feeling the weight of the commitment settle on his shoulders. "Ramir deserves that much."

"Good. Just... stay safe out there, man. And keep an eye on Ayanna too, her fuckin' cop buddies are all over us down here," Nate warned before ending the call.

As Don hung up the phone, he couldn't shake the feeling that the world was closing in on him. With Ramir's death, the war against the Munoz Cartel, and the uncertainty surrounding Nicolas as their drug distributor, it felt like everything was spiraling out of control.

But one thing was clear: he had to be there for Ramir's funeral. That much he owed to his fallen brother.

Don stood by the window, the cool New Jersey air seeping through the glass and chilling him to his core. His mind raced with thoughts of money, revenge, and betrayal. He rubbed his temples, feeling the weight of it all pushing down on him.

"Something wrong?" Ayanna asked softly, her dark eyes searching his face for any sign of what was going on behind those troubled eyes.

"Atlanta PD's been sniffin' around," he sighed, turning to face her. "I need to know what they got on us."

Ayanna hesitated, biting her lip as she considered her next words carefully. "They been tryna build a case against the Street Kings for years now. They think y'all involved in some heavy shit – drug trafficking, gun running, even murder."

"Damn," Don muttered, rubbing his chin thoughtfully. "How close they gettin'?"

"Hard to say for sure. But they still lack solid evidence," Ayanna replied, her voice laced with concern. "You gotta be careful, Don. One slip-up and everything could come crashing down."

Don nodded, knowing full well the stakes that hung in the balance. He walked over to Ayanna, taking her hands in his. "What about us, Ayanna? What we gonna do when this is all over?"

"Depends on what you want, Don," she whispered, looking deep into his eyes. "I got kicked off the force 'cause I couldn't stand watching them tear you apart. If you want me by your side, that's where I'll be."

"I want that more than anything," Don admitted, his heart pounding in his chest. "But there's somethin' else I gotta take care of first before we leave. I made a deal with Big Al to have the first building up and running before I head back home."

"That man ain't nothin' but trouble," Ayanna warned, her eyes narrowing in suspicion. "You sure you can trust him?"

"Big Al's deeper in this than any of us," Don explained, squeezing her hands reassuringly. "He got contacts and resources. If we gonna survive this war and come out on top, we need him on our side."

Ayanna sighed, nodding slowly as she mulled over his words. "Okay, Don. But don't forget why you in this game in the first place. You wanted to make things better for your people, not end up like one of these power-hungry fools."

"Don't worry," Don said, pulling her close and pressing his lips to her forehead. "I ain't gonna lose sight of what's important. We gonna build an empire together, and ain't nobody gonna tear it down."

As they stood there, wrapped in each other's arms, Don felt a small glimmer of hope amidst the chaos that surrounded them. Despite the darkness that loomed on the horizon, there was still a chance for them to forge a brighter future – together.

As the evening shadows draped over the room, Don couldn't help but notice the way Ayanna's eyes seemed to glow in the dim light. They'd been talking for hours, and their voices had grown softer, more intimate. It was as if they were sharing secrets only they could understand.

"Ya know," Ayanna began, leaning back against the couch, her legs folded under her. "I never thought I'd find myself feelin' this way 'bout someone like you."

Don shifted his weight on the cushions, mirroring her relaxed posture. He looked deep into her eyes, feeling an unspoken bond strengthening between them. "What you mean, someone like me?" he asked, a playful grin tugging at the corners of his mouth.

"A Street King like you, all rough around the edges," she teased, nudging him with her foot. "But underneath all that tough exterior, you got a heart of gold."

He chuckled, feeling the warmth spread through his chest. "And what 'bout you, huh? A cop – or, well, ex-cop – fallin' for a guy like me. Ain't that breakin' some kind of rule?"

"Rules are meant to be broken... sometimes" Ayanna said, her voice soft and low. She reached out, her fingers brushing up against his hand, sending a thrill down his spine. "I ain't gonna lie, it's scary as hell. But somethin' tells me it's worth it."

"Scary for me too, baby girl," Don admitted, interlacing his fingers with hers. "But I ain't never felt nothin' like this before. You make me wanna be a better man, do right by you and everyone else."

"Is that so?" Ayanna asked, her eyes twinkling. "So, what now?"

"Now we take this one step at a time," he replied, his voice firm and resolute. "We gonna face whatever comes our way together. You got me?"

"Got you," she echoed, her lips curving into a genuine smile.

A comfortable silence settled between them, their fingers still entwined. Don's mind raced with thoughts of the future – a future in which he and Ayanna could build something real, something untainted by the bloodshed and betrayal that had become all too familiar. It was a dream they both wanted to believe in, no matter how distant it seemed.

"Promise me something, Don" Ayanna whispered, her gaze locked onto his.

"This is like your fifth promise," he joked, his tone serious.

Ayanna smiled. "Promise me we'll never let this world break us apart again," she said, her voice cracking ever so slightly.

"I promise" he vowed, sealing the pact with a gentle kiss on her hand. "Together, we're unstoppable."

And at that moment, as their eyes met and held, Don knew that he'd found something worth fighting for, even as the storm of violence and retribution threatened to engulf them all.

The room was faintly lit, an orange glow from the streetlights outside casting long shadows across the walls. Don and Ayanna sat side by side on the edge of the bed, the weight of their conversation still hanging heavy in the air. It was as if the world outside had ceased to exist, leaving only the two of them and the electric current that seemed to crackle between them.

"Can I be honest with you?" Ayanna asked, her voice barely a whisper. She looked at Don, her dark eyes wide and vulnerable.

"Of course," he replied, his own voice low and steady.

"I've wanted you for so long," she admitted, her cheeks flushing with a mix of embarrassment and desire. "But I never thought we'd find ourselves here, like this."

"Me neither, but life's full of surprises," Don said, the corner of his mouth quirking up into a half-smile. "And I ain't complainin'."

He reached out to brush a strand of hair behind her ear, his fingers lingering on her smooth skin. He could feel her heart pounding beneath his touch, matching the racing beat of his own. The heat between them was undeniable, a magnetic pull that drew them closer with every passing second.

"Neither am I," Ayanna murmured, her breath hitching as Don's hand moved from her cheek to her neck, feeling the pulse point there. She met his gaze, her eyes filled with a hunger that mirrored his own.

"Show me how much you want me," Don challenged, his voice thick with lust.

Ayanna responded by pressing her lips to his, her hands reaching up to tangle in his hair. Their mouths melded together, their tongues tangled in a dance as old as time. With each heated exchange, the sexual tension between them grew, threatening to consume them both.

Don pulled back slightly, his breath ragged. "I need you" he rasped, his voice strained with need.

"Then take me" Ayanna whispered, the fire in her eyes blazing brighter than ever before.

The floodgates broke, and Don's hands were suddenly everywhere – trailing down her back, gripping her hips, tracing the curve of her breasts through the thin fabric of her shirt. Ayanna's own fingers were just as busy, working to undo the buttons of his shirt with a feverish urgency.

Their clothes were discarded in a haphazard pile on the floor, their bodies pressed tightly together as they fell back onto the bed. The sheets were cool against their heated skin, but neither seemed to notice or care. All that mattered was the connection between them, the insatiable desire that drove them onward. As they moved together, Don and Ayanna seemed to transcend time and space, lost in the swirling vortex of their passion. Every touch, every kiss, every whispered word sent shockwaves through their bodies, igniting their souls in a blaze of ecstasy.

Ayanna's moans filled the room, music to Don's ears as he drove her closer and closer to the edge. He could feel the tremors racking her body, the telltale sign of her impending release. With one final thrust, she shattered, screaming his name as she rode the waves of her orgasm.

Don wasn't far behind, his own release exploding through him like a supernova. He collapsed onto Ayanna's chest, the sweat and heat of their bodies melding together in a perfect union.

For a few moments, they simply laid there, panting and gasping for air. Then, Don lifted himself up and looked down at Ayanna, his eyes filled with a mix of adoration and desire.

As they came together, the outside world ceased to exist once more. There was only Don and Ayanna, two souls finding solace in each other amidst the storm of chaos that threatened to tear them apart.

"Wow," Don panted in the aftermath, sweat glistening on his brow as he stared up at the ceiling. He could feel Ayanna's warm body beside him, her chest rising and falling in time with his own labored breaths.

In the silence that followed, Don's thoughts turned inward, tangling themselves into knots of uncertainty and longing. He had found something special with Ayanna, but the ghost of Isabella still haunted him, her memory a bittersweet reminder of what might have been. As he lay there, caught between past and present, Don couldn't shake the feeling that the path ahead was fraught with danger and heartache.

But for now, as he pulled Ayanna closer and let her warmth envelop him, Don allowed himself to live in the moment, cherishing the bond they'd forged and praying it was strong enough to withstand the storm that was surely on its way.

Don and Ayanna lay entwined in the sleazy motel room, the flickering bulb from a lamp providing them with less than sufficient lighting. The scent of their passion hung heavily in the air, a mixture of sweat, desire, and something deeper.

"Yo, that was... somethin' else," Don whispered, his voice rough with raw emotion. His fingers traced lazy patterns on Ayanna's bare skin, feeling the goosebumps rising beneath his touch.

"Never knew it could be like this, Don," Ayanna murmured, her eyes locked onto his as she spoke the truth they both felt, but were afraid to say aloud.

"Me neither, ma." Don smiled weakly, the weight of the world pressing down on him. He couldn't shake off the nagging thoughts that swirled around his mind like vultures circling their prey.

"Hey, you good?" Ayanna asked, sensing the turmoil within him. She propped herself up on one elbow, her dark curls framing her face.

Don hesitated before answering, his gaze drifting to the ceiling as he tried to put words to the chaos inside his head. "I dunno, Ayanna. I'm just..." He trailed off, struggling to find the right words.

"Confused?" she suggested, understanding flashing in her eyes.

"Exactly," he admitted, running a hand through his hair. "Like, we got this thing between us, and it's real, but I can't help thinkin' 'bout Isabella too."

"Isabella?" Ayanna questioned, her tone neutral, though the hurt in her eyes betrayed her.

"Yea" Don sighed. "She been on my mind lately, and I ain't sure what it all means."

"Look," Ayanna began, her voice firm but gentle. "What we got is special, no doubt, but I already told you that I ain't gonna force you into something you ain't ready for. If Isabella is who you want, then go be with her. Just know that I'm here if you need me."

"Damn, Ayanna" Don whispered, touched by her selflessness. "You really somethin' else, you know that?"

"Yea" she replied, a sad smile playing on her lips. "I know."

Their eyes met once more, the unspoken words hanging heavily in the air between them. It was clear that both their hearts were at stake, and whatever decision Don made would have lasting consequences.

As the night wore on, Don found himself unable to shake the confusion that gripped him. He was torn between the two women, unsure of what the future held, and fearful of making the wrong choice.

"Life ain't never easy, is it?" he murmured to himself, staring out the window at the city below. The streets were dark and unforgiving, much like the path that lay ahead of him.

"Sometimes, no," Ayanna whispered, placing a comforting hand on his arm. "But together, we can face whatever comes our way."

And as they lay there, wrapped in each other's arms, Don couldn't help but wonder if that would be enough to see them through the storm that was fast approaching.

Chapter 9

The sunlight streamed through the blinds, casting a warm glow on Don as he prepared coffee for himself and Ayanna. The scent of freshly brewed java filled the room, mingling with the lingering scent of their passionate night together. He couldn't help but smile as he recalled the way her body had felt pressed against his, and how they had moved in sync like two parts of a single machine.

"Morning," Ayanna murmured, voice still thick with sleep as she emerged from the bedroom, wearing nothing but one of Don's shirts. She leaned against the counter, watching him with a sly grin. "You make a mean cup of coffee."

"Only the best for you, baby girl," Don replied, handing her a steaming mug. Their fingers brushed briefly, sending a jolt of electricity through him. He knew they had business to attend to, but part of him wanted nothing more than to pull her back into bed and lose themselves in each other once more.

"Thanks," she said, taking a sip of the coffee and giving him an appreciative nod. "So, what do you have planned for us today?"

"We are gonna meet with some contractors," Don confirmed, grabbing his own cup and taking a swig. "Big Al wants us to get these jewelry stores up and running ASAP. We need to make sure the remodeling goes smoothly so we can start moving them diamonds legit."

They got dressed and climbed into Don's sleek black Mercedes, the leather seats still warm from the sun beating down on the car. As they cruised through the streets of Jersey, Don laid out the specifics for Ayanna.

"Big Al's got three buildings that need renovation. One's gonna be all high-end, real classy – chandeliers, marble floors, the works. The second one's gonna cater to the middle market – still nice, but not too flashy. And the third is gonna be a mix – something for everyone, you know?"

"Sounds like yall got it all figured out," Ayanna said, her eyes scanning the passing scenery.

"The man knows what he wants," Don agreed, gripping the steering wheel tightly. "He told me that once we get these stores up and runnin', we're gonna have access to some of the most valuable diamonds in the world. We just gotta make sure everything goes according to plan."

As they continued on their way to meet with the contractors, Don couldn't help but glance over at Ayanna from time to time. He knew they were treading on dangerous ground – a former cop and a hustler, trying to navigate the treacherous waters of Atlanta's and New Jersey's criminal underworlds together. But something about her made him believe it was all worth it – that maybe, just maybe, they could find a way to make it work.

"I need a guarantee from you," he said suddenly, his voice soft and serious.

"Anything," Ayanna replied, turning her gaze to meet his.

"You gotta make sure that no matter what happens, we'll always have each other's backs. That we'll fight through whatever life throws at us, together, even when it comes to dealing with your old colleagues."

"Always," she whispered, reaching over to squeeze his hand as they sped down the highway, their future uncertain but their bond unbreakable.

Don pulled up to the main site, the sound of hammers and drills filling the air as workers hustled about. He scanned the area, his eyes landing on a Lorenzo in a tailored suit, barking orders with a thick Italian accent.

"Stay close," Don told Ayanna as they got out of the car. "Lorenzo ain't nothin' to play with. It looks like he's all business."

"Got it," she replied, following Don as he approached Lorenzo.

"Ah, Don," Lorenzo greeted him with a firm handshake. "Glad you could make it. Let me introduce you to the head contractor, Tony. He'll be handling the renovations for these properties." Lorenzo gestured to a burly man in a hard hat.

"Nice to meet you, Tony," Don said, shaking the contractor's hand.

"Likewise," Tony replied, wiping sweat from his brow. "We're making good progress here. Should have these places looking like top-notch jewelry stores in no time."

"Good," Don nodded, scanning the blueprints spread out on a nearby table. "Big Al's countin' on us to get this done right."

Lorenzo lit a cigar, taking a deep drag before speaking. "I've been keeping an eye on everything, making sure the workers stay on schedule and follow the design plans. As long as there are no surprises, we should be fine."

"Speaking of surprises, we've been having some personnel issues down in Atlanta," Don admitted, rubbing the back of his neck. "I gotta head back tomorrow for a funeral."

"Understood," Lorenzo said, exhaling smoke through his nostrils. "You go do what you have to do. We'll handle things here."

"Appreciate it," Don replied, his eyes flicking to Ayanna for a moment. He could tell she was uneasy, but she kept her composure.

"Look," Lorenzo continued, "we're all in this together. Big Al's got our backs, and we got his. We just need to stick to the plan and make sure these stores are up and running as smoothly as possible."

"Bet," Don agreed, clapping Lorenzo on the shoulder. "We ain't gonna let Big Al down."

"Not all all," Lorenzo nodded. "Now, let's get back to work. Time is money."

As they turned their attention back to the blueprints and the ongoing construction, Don couldn't help but wonder if they were truly prepared for the challenges that lay ahead. But he knew one thing for certain – he'd do whatever it took to protect those he cared about, even if it meant risking everything.

"Look, Don," Lorenzo said, glancing around to ensure they had some privacy. "Big Al told me that you've been having issues in Atlanta and that he agreed to give you a small army of our men to help deal with that problem. I just want you to know that we are both still upset about the attempt on your life and feel terrible. I want to make it right, so I'll be sending you a group of our most loyal Italian soldiers to accompany you and ensure your safety at the funeral."

"A group?" Don raised an eyebrow.

"Ten men, all trained in combat and with experience in the streets," Lorenzo explained. "They'll follow you to hell and back, no questions asked."

"Cool," Don muttered, looking at Ayanna, who seemed uneasy about the news. "I appreciate yall for lookin' out for me like that, but we gotta be careful. I don't want any more blood on my hands and I don't want any snakes around me."

"I assumed you would say that." Lorenzo nodded. "But these guys are the best and you won't have any problems out of them. They'll help you take care of your problems once and for all."

"If you say so," Don agreed reluctantly. "Let's give this a shot. It can't hurt to have extra muscle, especially now."

Just then, the sound of high heels clicking against the concrete floor echoed through the building. Don and Ayanna turned to see Isabella walking towards them, holding a bottle of champagne and a box of glasses, with a confident smile plastered on her face.

"Thought we could use some bubbly to celebrate our progress," she announced, stopping in front of them.

"Isabella," Don said, taken aback by her sudden appearance. Ayanna stiffened beside him, her eyes narrowing as she regarded the beautiful Italian woman.

"Hey, Donnie," Isabella purred, her gaze lingering on him before flicking over to Ayanna. "Who's your friend?"

"Isabella, this is Ayanna," Don introduced them, trying to diffuse the tension. "Ayanna, this is Isabella. She is a diamond expert for Big Al."

"Nice to meet you," Ayanna said through gritted teeth, clearly not pleased by Isabella's presence.

"Likewise," Isabella replied, her eyes locked onto Ayanna's in a silent challenge. "I just wanted to drop by and make sure everything's going according to plan."

"Everything's on track," Don assured her, sensing the growing tension between the two women. "We're doin' our best to get these stores up and runnin' as soon as possible."

"Good," Isabella said, popping the cork off the champagne bottle. "Then let's toast to our success."

As she poured the champagne into three glasses, Don couldn't help but feel caught in the middle of an unspoken battle between Isabella and Ayanna. He knew he had to figure out a way to keep the peace, but with his impending trip back to Atlanta and the threat against the Street Kings looming, it wouldn't be easy. And with Big Al's men joining the fray, the stakes were higher than ever.

Don handed his glass to Ayanna, then poured a fourth glass of bubbly. Isabella scoffed at his actions and rolled her eyes at Ayanna. "Here's to successful partnerships that will make us all rich," Don announced, raising his glass. The others raised their glasses too, acknowledging the toast.

The smell of fresh paint lingered in the air as Don watched Isabella strut across the unfinished floor, her heels clicking on the concrete. She pointed at various spots in the store, rattling off the equipment that would be needed to complete the project.

"Over here," she said, her voice dripping with confidence, "we're gonna need a state-of-the-art security system. Cameras, motion sensors, the works. And right there," she gestured to another corner, "that's where we'll put the vault. Big Al wants it reinforced with steel and concrete, you know, to protect his investments."

"Sounds like we got our work cut out for us," Don muttered, taking in the scope of the project. He glanced over at Ayanna, who was silently observing the exchange between him and Isabella, her arms crossed defensively.

"Indeed," Lorenzo chimed in, his eyes never leaving Isabella. "But with all of us working together, I'm sure we can make this happen."

"Here, here!" Isabella exclaimed, raising her champagne glass. "To the future success of Big Al's jewelry empire!"

As they clinked their glasses together, Don couldn't help but notice the rising tension between Isabella and Ayanna. The two women exchanged terse smiles, their eyes locked in a silent battle of wills.

"Let's get back to work," Lorenzo said, breaking the uneasy silence. "Time is money, after all."

"Right," Don agreed, setting down his empty champagne glass. He shot a quick glance at Ayanna, trying to gauge her thoughts, but her face remained impassive. As he turned to follow Lorenzo and Isabella, he felt Ayanna's hand on his arm.

"Be careful, Don," she whispered, her eyes filled with concern. "I don't trust her."

Don nodded, understanding the unspoken warning. With so much at stake, he couldn't afford to let his guard down, not even around those who seemed to be on his side. As they continued their walk-through of the building, Don made a silent vow to himself that he would do whatever it took to protect his loved ones and bring his enemies to justice, no matter the cost.

"Remember," Isabella called out over her shoulder as they left the store, "we're all on the same team."

Yes we are, Don thought, his eyes following Isabella's swaying hips as she sauntered away. But with so much tension brewing between the people who were supposed to be on his side, he couldn't help but wonder how long their fragile alliance would hold.

As they walked through the building, Lorenzo slapped Don on the back with a grin that didn't quite reach his eyes. "Don, my man, you're like a King of Diamonds around here. You got this whole operation shining."

"The King of Diamonds?" Don chuckled, taking in the compliment as he surveyed the progress they'd made. The nickname suited him – he was a master at turning rough stones into priceless gems, both in business and in life.

"Damn right," Lorenzo continued. "You've got the Midas touch, making everything you touch turn to gold. Or should I say diamonds?" He laughed, but there was an undertone of envy in his voice.

"Appreciate that, Lorenzo," Don replied, feeling the weight of the title settle onto his shoulders. There was no room for error, not if he wanted to maintain control over the empire he'd built.

As the group moved further into the space, Isabella's gaze kept flickering between Ayanna and Don. Eventually, she pulled Don aside, her dark eyes questioning. "So, who is she? And where did she suddenly come from?"

"Long story short, she's been by my side since day one in Atlanta," Don explained, keeping his voice low so as not to draw attention. "We've been through some heavy stuff together, and she's proved herself time and time again."

"Atlanta, huh?" Isabella said, her expression hardening. "I heard about the trouble down there. I also heard that you're leaving soon?"

"Tomorrow," Don confirmed, bracing himself for Isabella's reaction. "Got to handle some business, put things back in order."

"Then let me come with you," she said, her face softening slightly. "I can help."

"Look, Isabella, I appreciate the offer, but I need you here," Don told her firmly, hoping she would understand. "You're the only one who knows this jewelry game from top to bottom. I can't have these stores running without someone making sure that they shine."

"Fine," Isabella sighed, clearly disappointed but accepting his decision. "Just be careful, Don. I don't want anything to happen to you."

"I got you," he said, giving her a reassuring smile. But as he turned away to rejoin Ayanna and Lorenzo, Don couldn't shake the feeling that his path was leading him towards more danger than he'd ever faced before.

Isabella's eyes shimmered like the diamonds that she wore around her neck, but her lips pressed into a thin line. She nodded curtly. "I'll do it. I'll oversee the stores." Then, with a sad smile, she added, "I'll do it for the King of Diamonds."

Don watched as she stormed out of the building, his heart heavy. He knew she cared, maybe even loved him, but there was no time for that now. With a deep breath, he turned back to Ayanna and Lorenzo. Their expressions were a mix of concern and determination.

"Business aside," Lorenzo said, folding his arms across his broad chest. "How are you holding up?"

"Been better," Don admitted, glancing briefly at Ayanna. She gave him a small smile but didn't say anything.

"Hey, it's all good," Lorenzo reassured them. "You know we are here for you. And I'll make sure everything runs smoothly here while you take care of things down south."

"Thank you," Don said, nodding in gratitude. He looked over at Ayanna, who seemed lost in thought. "Aye, you cool?"

"Yea, just... I can't believe we gotta deal with street nonsense again," she sighed, rubbing her temples. "But ain't nothin' we can't handle, right?"

"Right," Don agreed, putting a reassuring hand on her shoulder. "We've been through worse. We'll get through this too."

"Speaking of which," Lorenzo interjected, pulling out a thick manila envelope from his jacket. "Here's some cash for Ayanna. Just a little thank you from the boss for putting your name on the paperwork. There will be a lot more where that came from."

"Wow, thank you so much," Ayanna mumbled, grabbing the thick envelope. She had never had this much money in her life. It was almost triple her annual salary from the police department.

"Yeah, thanks for this," Don said, gratefully accepting the envelope.

"Anything for family," Lorenzo replied, clapping him on the back. "Now go on, get ready for your trip. We'll handle things here."

As they left the building, Don couldn't help but notice the lingering scent of Isabella's perfume. It was like a ghost, haunting him as he prepared to face the demons in Atlanta. But there was no turning back now – the King of Diamonds had a score to settle, and he'd be damned if he let anything, or anyone, stand in his way.

Chapter 10

The funeral for Ramir was a grand affair, befitting a man of his loyalty and dedication. Mourners filed into the lavish church, its stained-glass windows shimmering as the raindrops splattered against them like tears from the heavens. The scent of roses filled the air, mingling with the somber whispers of those who had come to pay their respects.

The pews were lined with friends, family, and members of the Street Kings, each dressed in their finest black and gold attire. At the front of the church, an elaborate casket draped in opulence held the remains of the fallen soldier. Despite the danger that lurked in the streets, the dedication of those in attendance was evident – they had shown up to honor the memory of a man who had given everything for the cause.

Don and Ayanna arrived together, stepping out of a sleek black car as the rain poured down around them. The water streamed over his tailored suit and her elegant black dress and did nothing but dampen their spirits.

Their eyes were red-rimmed from shedding tears, and their faces were etched with pain. They clung to one another, drawing strength from each other's presence as they prepared to face the heartache inside the church.

"Yo, this ain't right, Ayanna," Don muttered, his voice cracking with grief. "Ramir deserved better than this. He deserved to grow old."

"Life ain't fair sometimes, Don," Ayanna replied softly, trying to comfort him even as she fought back her own tears. "But we're here for him now, and that's what matters."

As they entered the church, the weight of their loss hung heavy on their shoulders. The sound of the organ playing a mournful melody enveloped them, echoing through the vaulted ceilings like a haunting commemoration of what had been taken from them. But even in the midst of their sorrow, there was a sense of determination and unity among the mourners – a shared understanding that Ramir's death would not be in vain.

Don's new Italian crew, dressed in sleek black suits, escorted him and Ayanna inside the church. Their presence was intimidating, a reminder of the dangerous world they were all a part of. Ayanna scanned the crowd as they walked down the aisle, her investigative instincts kicking in. She suddenly spotted a few familiar faces among the mourners – undercover cops she had once worked with.

"Oh fuck," she whispered to Don, nodding discreetly toward the men. "Looks like my old colleagues decided to pay their respects too."

Don's jaw clenched as he glanced at the undercover officers, their expressions a mix of guilt and determination. They made eye contact with Ayanna, acknowledging her with blank stares and disgusting glares before looking away. The emotional conflict stirred within Ayanna, torn between her past obligations to the badge and present loyalty to Don.

Ayanna knew that the police department already suspected her of switching sides and now they had their confirmation. She struggled with her new reality because she knew how hard she worked when she was on the force. Love had a funny way of changing your life and for her, it was a dramatic change.

"Stay focused, babe," Don murmured, his hand tightening around hers. "We're here for Ramir."

As they reached their seats, the doors opened again, drawing everyone's attention. Cash and Reana entered; their heads held high despite the pain that shadowed their eyes. Behind them came a group of women, all donning long black dresses. Don didn't recognize any of the women and was confused as to what their relationship was to his cousin. *Maybe they're Jamaicans*, he thought as his eyes stayed trained on them.

Ramir's family filed in next, their grief palpable. His mother clutched a tissue tightly, tears streaming down her face as she was guided to a seat by Ramir's younger sister. Don's heart ached for them, knowing their lives would never be the same.

Ace was the last to enter, flanked by some of his local goons, some of their attire a stark contrast to the somber atmosphere. Each member wore a custom hoodie emblazoned with Ramir's face and the words "Rest in Power" inscribed below it, a bold statement that refused to let Ramir's memory fade. Don watched as Ace walked directly to the casket to pay his respects.

"Lord, help us," Ayanna whispered, her voice barely audible amidst the muffled sobs and distant thunder outside. Her thoughts were a whirlwind of emotions – anger, sadness, and an overwhelming sense of responsibility for the events that had led them here.

"Remember, Ayanna," Don said softly, his eyes locked on the closed casket at the front of the church. "We'll make this right. For Ramir, for all of us."

As the pastor began to speak, a tense stillness filled the air, each person in the room united by grief and the unspoken promise of retribution. The storm brewing outside mirrored the turmoil within the church, setting the stage for a confrontation that would shake the foundations of their world.

The pastor's words were barely audible over the sound of thunder and organs, as he began the funeral rites. The tension in the church was a living, breathing entity, and Don couldn't help but feel that something was about to snap.

"Let us pray for Ramir's soul," the pastor intoned, raising his hands heavenward. And that's when all hell broke loose.

The heavy wooden doors of the church burst open with a splintering crash, revealing Deuce and a dozen heavily armed Colombian soldiers. Their faces were cold and menacing, and their intentions clear. Time seemed to slow as their weapons were raised, the deadly glint of metal catching the dim candlelight.

"Everybody down!" Ayanna shouted, her instincts kicking in as she dove for cover. The mourners screamed and scattered like frightened birds, some crouching low while others made desperate attempts to flee.

"Get down, get down!" Cash yelled from the back, grabbing Reana's arm and pulling her to the floor, shielding her body with his own.

"Protect my family!" Ace commanded his crew, readying themselves for the inevitable firefight. They had sworn loyalty to him, and they would prove it now in the most violent way possible.

"Traitors!" Deuce spat, his eyes locked on Ace. "You think you can betray us and live? Ramir was just the beginning!"

Gunfire erupted, the deafening sound ricocheting off the church's stone walls. "Police, drop your weapons," someone ordered, but no one complied. The officers announced themselves, drawing their firearms to protect the innocent but now drawing attention from the Colombians. The scene was chaotic as the Colombians and undercover cops exchanged volleys of bullets. Pews shattered under the onslaught, sending splinters of wood flying through the air.

"Damn it, I knew this was coming," Don thought, his pulse pounding in his ears. "But not here, not now." He glanced at Ayanna, who was crouched nearby, her expression a mixture of fear and determination. *I gotta keep her safe.*

"Stay down, baby," he murmured to her, his voice barely audible over the chaos. "I got you."

"Deuce, you piece of shit!" Ace shouted, firing off rounds in the direction of the attackers. "You ain't gonna get away with this!"

"Watch me!" Deuce snarled, returning fire with deadly precision.

"Lord, please protect us," Ayanna prayed silently, her hands shaking as she clutched her weapon. "Not just me and Don, but everyone here. This madness has to end."

As the chaos in the church escalated, Don's Italian crew sprang into action. With well-rehearsed precision, they moved to protect their new leader and Ayanna, shielding them from the deadly crossfire.

"Stay close, boss," Marco shouted, his thick Italian accent tangled with the sound of gunfire. He fired off several shots at the Colombian soldiers, providing cover for Don and Ayanna as the Italians covered them and made their way towards a side exit.

"Keep moving, baby girl," Don urged Ayanna, pushing her forward even as she tried to catch her breath. His heart raced, adrenaline pumping through him, but one thought dominated his mind: he had to keep her safe.

Outside, the rain poured down mercilessly, turning the ground into a muddy mess. As they emerged from the church, Don, Ayanna, and the Italians were met by two Colombians lying in wait.

"Look who we got here," one of them sneered, leveling his gun at Don. "Thought you could escape, huh?"

"Y'all ain't going nowhere," the other added, aiming at Ayanna.

"Shit," Don muttered under his breath, halting and raising his hands to surrender.

"Boss, we'll handle this," Marco insisted, stepping in front of Don as one of the other Italians stepped in front of Ayanna. The Italians exchanged quick nods as they raised their weapons, their eyes never leaving the enemy. They knew their mission – ensuring the safety of Don and Ayanna was paramount.

"Y'all really think you can take us?" The first Colombian laughed, his finger hovering over the trigger.

"Try it and see," Marco challenged, his own gun pointed squarely at the man's chest. "But I promise you, it won't end well."

"Enough talk!" Don barked, his anger spilling over. "Let's finish this!"

"Your funeral will be next," the second Colombian taunted before opening fire.

"Down!" Don shouted, pushing Ayanna to the ground and covering her with his body. Her heart pounded in her chest, fear and determination coursing through her veins.

"Get 'em!" Marco ordered, his voice raw with fury. The Italians returned fire, engaging the Colombians in a deadly dance of bullets and blood.

"Stay down, baby," Don whispered to Ayanna, his eyes flicking between her and the battle unfolding before them. "We're gonna make it out of this."

"Damn right we are," she replied, gritting her teeth. "They picked the wrong people to mess with."

"Got 'em!" Marco bellowed, as the first Colombian crumpled to the ground. His gun roared, echoing with lethal intention. The second Colombian met a similar fate as someone put a bullet directly between his eyes.

"Three o'clock!" Ayanna warned, her eyes darting around the chaotic scene, catching sight of another Colombian trying to flank them. He was met by a hail of bullets from one of Don's Italian crew members, his body jerking violently as he collapsed.

"Move!" Don commanded, his voice laced with urgency. He and Ayanna scrambled to their feet, following behind the Italians as they pressed forward through the parking lot. Ayanna's old instincts kicked in as she grabbed one of the guns that were dropped by their fallen enemies. The rain grew heavier, splattering against the asphalt like tiny explosions.

"Watch our six!" Marco yelled, his pistol aimed at a shadowy figure ducking between cars. His men's instincts flared, and one fired off a shot, narrowly missing the dark figure but forcing him back into hiding.

"Shit, this is intense," Don muttered, wiping rain and sweat from his brow. He glanced at Ayanna, her face etched with determination. She had her weapon gripped tightly in her hand, scanning their surroundings for any further threats.

"The car is just up ahead," Marco announced, pointing towards an inconspicuous black sedan parked strategically near the exit.

"Good, let's get outta here," Don replied, tightening his hold on Ayanna's hand as they picked up speed. The sounds of sirens could be heard in the distance.

"Boss, you two go," Marco urged, holding his position while the rest of the Italians provided cover fire. "We'll handle things here."

"Be careful," Don cautioned, his concern evident. Despite the odds stacked against them, he couldn't forget the loyalty and dedication of his crew.

"Of course," Marco grinned, before turning his attention back to the approaching danger.

"Come on," Ayanna said, giving Don's hand a reassuring squeeze as they sprinted towards the waiting sedan. She could feel her heart pounding, adrenaline fueling her every move.

"Stay low," Don instructed, throwing open the passenger door and helping Ayanna inside. He made his way around to the driver's side, sliding into the seat with practiced ease. He started the engine, the roar of the V8 drowning out the sounds of gunfire behind them.

"No!" Ayanna shouted, her eyes wide as she saw a Colombian soldier emerge from behind another car that pulled in front of theirs, aiming straight for Marco. "Marco!" Ayanna yelled out the window, alerting him to the danger. He spun around just in time to take out the would-be attacker, firing off a shot that slammed into the assailant's chest.

"Thanks for the heads up," Marco gasped, his voice strained. "We'll meet you at the rendezvous point."

"Be safe," Don warned, glancing in the rearview mirror as the church compound faded into the distance. The evening rain continued to pour down, washing away the blood and violence that had marred Ramir's final farewell.

"Damn," Ayanna murmured, her body trembling from the rush of it all. "We made it out."

"Only by the skin of our teeth," Don admitted, gripping the steering wheel tightly. "But we're not out of this yet, baby."

"Whatever happens next," she replied, her voice resolute, "we'll be ready for it."

Don's heart pounded in his ears as he navigated the black BMW through Atlanta's rain-soaked streets, a sharp contrast to the sudden calmness that Ayanna projected. He could still hear the distant echoes of gunfire and the anguished screams of those caught in the crossfire. The assault of sounds mingled with the memories of Ramir's once peaceful funeral, now stained by violence.

"Fuck," Don muttered under his breath, shaking his head at the devastation left behind. "This shit ain't over."

Ayanna reached over to squeeze Don's hand, her expression a mixture of concern and determination. "We'll get through this," she assured him, her voice thick with emotion.

He continued driving, still not feeling completely safe despite having several miles between them and the church. He pulled out his phone. "Yo, is everybody good?" Don asked in a voice message, desperate for news on his crew and their allies.

"We all made it out, boss," Marco responded in a message of his own, his voice tense but steady. "There were a lot of soldiers down on both sides. And I think there were cops inside of the church too."

"Shit..." Don clenched his jaw, feeling the weight of each life lost like an anchor around his neck. He knew that this violent reality was part of the life they had chosen, but it never got any easier.

"Is there any word from Cash?" Ayanna inquired, her concern rising above the chaos that surrounded them.

"Nothing yet," Don replied, his grip tightening on the steering wheel. "But I'm sure he'll be in touch soon."

As they raced towards the rendezvous point, the adrenaline began to subside, replaced by fear and uncertainty. They were far from safe, and repercussions would inevitably follow the carnage that had erupted during Ramir's funeral. The Street Kings and their enemies were more entwined than ever, and the lines between loyalty and betrayal blurred even further.

"Whatever happens," Don said, his voice low and resolute, "we'll figure it out."

"Right," Ayanna agreed, her hand now gripping Don's leg tightly. "Together."

The sound of gunfire still echoed in the distance, a lingering reminder of the danger that loomed over them. But despite the terror and uncertainty that awaited them, Don and Ayanna were determined to face it head-on, their resolve unshaken and their loyalty unwavering. The storm may have passed for now, but he knew that darker clouds were gathering, promising even more violence and chaos in the days to come.

The End

AVAILABLE NOW

AVAILABLE NOW

AVAILABLE NOW

AVAILABLE NOW

AVAILABLE NOW

COMING SOON...

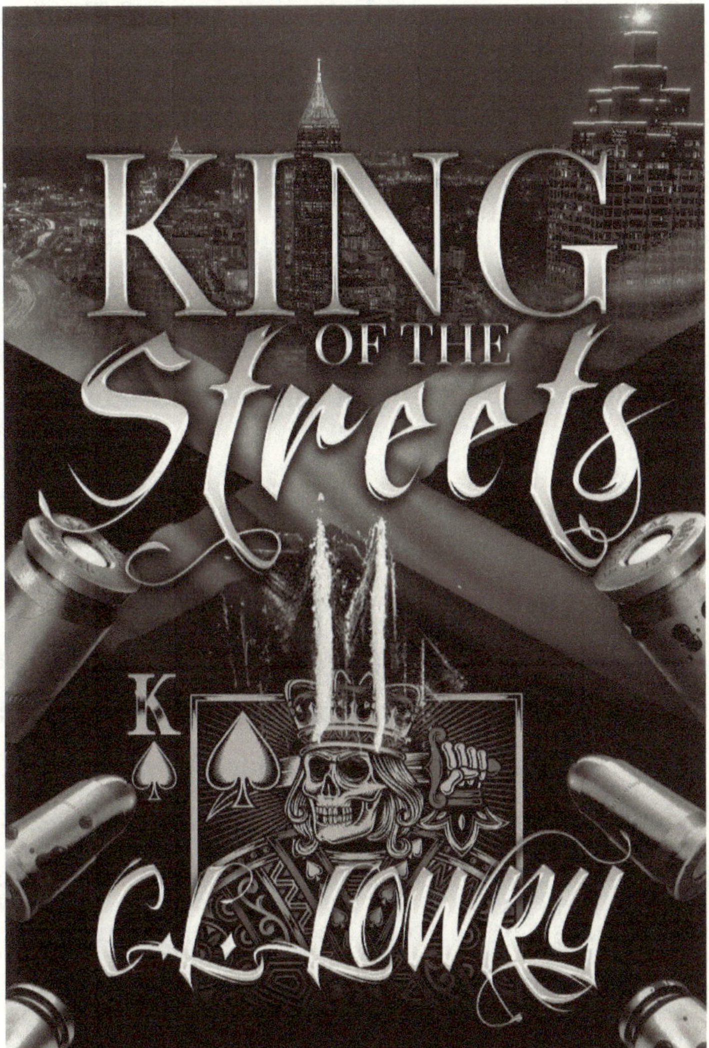

ABOUT THE AUTHOR

C.L. Lowry is an award-winning author and filmmaker. Although he prides himself as being a prolific crime novelist, his pen game is versatile and allows him to navigate through multiple genres. Lowry was born and raised in Philadelphia, Pennsylvania but his family roots trace back to the beautiful island of Barbados, West Indies. Lowry uses his life experiences and creativity to demand his readers' attention with realistic scenarios throughout his stories.

When he isn't penning a page-turning novel, Lowry is behind the camera creating high-quality films under his production company, Black Lens Cinema. Lowry is also the host of the Fiction Addiction Podcast, where he interviews authors, filmmakers, and other creatives. Sign up for Lowry's spam-free newsletter to learn more about future releases, sneak peeks, special offers, and bonus content. Subscribers will also receive access to exclusive giveaways. To sign up, visit his website at **www.authorcllowry.com**.

CREEDOM PUBLISHING COMPANY

Creedom Publishing is a fully incorporated publishing company. Much like our slogan "The Home of Creative Freedom," we are committed to providing new and upcoming authors with the resources and opportunity to share their creativity with the world.

Creedom Book Services is the parent company to Creedom Publishing Company. Under our publishing company, we provide quality books for readers of all ages. Whether it's the eye-catching childrens book series for young readers or the page-turning crime thrillers by award-winning author C.L. Lowry, every book under Creedom Publishing Company is worthy of being added to your library.

Our books are available for purchase on our site and eBooks are available through Amazon Kindle.

www.ingramcontent.com/pod-product-compliance
Lightning Source LLC
Chambersburg PA
CBHW022120170626
46808CB00002B/795